Victor K.C. is a Lawyer and Theologian. This is his first of three novels he calls "The Jesus Trilogy". The first is a creative critical look into Jesus in court. The second is on the very opposite of Jesus; the devil. And the climax of the trilogy is the world's best seller, the Bible, in court!

Jesus: Guilty or Innocent?

Victor K.C.

Trafford rev. 09/26/2011

 www.trafford.com

North America & international
toll-free: 1 888 232 4444 (USA & Canada)
phone: 250 383 6864 ♦ fax: 812 355 4082

To my children;

Dylan, Bob, Denver and Presley.

AUTH⊕R'S N⊕TE:

If you are looking for God check Good, but
if it is evil you seek, check the Devil!

Victor K.C.

Table of Contents

PR⊕L⊕GUE

It is true. Christian Cox tore his Bible and threw it in the fire. He watched the Bible burn like a sinner in hell. Having pulled down a crucifix from his wall, he threw it on the floor and trampled it with disdain. He then hastily grabbed his keys and rushed to his X D2 sports car without giving a thought to the heavy downpour. Like a mad man, he drove to California police headquarters breathing heavily and shaking with anger. The silence of the police station was disturbed as he burst open the entrance door fuming with rage and stared at the police officers.

'Take it easy sir. Can I help you?' asked one polite police officer.

'Yes you can. That is why I am here,' screamed Christian.

'Can you tell me what your problem is sir?'

Yes I can- and I will. I have read the Da Vinci Code and I am not going to let him get away with it,' he said furiously.

'Not let who get away with it?'

'I have been a Christian for forty years and I am disappointed to find out that Christianity is just a gigantic fraud. A lie. A cheat. A brainwash,' shouted Christian still trembling with anger.

'Relax sir. Take it is easy.'

'No officer. I have no time to waste. My two sons and daughter no longer go to church because I have failed to explain to them the Da Vinci questions. My whole forty years as a Christian have been reduced to nothing. My children now think I have been hiding the truth. Now I am jobless and faithless. Left naked. Useless.'

'I understand sir...'

'No you don't. I want to know if that girl, Mary Magdalene, was his girl friend. I want to know if he was having sex with her. I want to know whether he was just mortal man made divine by some narrow vote in some underground church meeting. I want to know ...'

'Sorry for interrupting you sir. You still have not told me who you want arrested.'

'O wretched man, open your eyes! I want him… him who has cheated me into Christianity. I want him… him who has brainwashed me with fake resurrection stories. I want him who has wasted my forty years as a Christian.'

'Oh holy shit, you do not mean…'

'Yes I do. I want Jesus Christ arrested dead or alive.'

CHAPTER 1

ARREST THE DEAD MAN

Great laughter erupted in the police headquarters when a police officer read what purported to be an arrest warrant for Jesus Christ. The warrant was dated 1st April 2011, duly signed by a Judge, with an order from the police chief that the warrant be executed.

It was a chilly Monday morning. Police officers who worked at police headquarters had all reported for duty except their boss. Little did they know that their boss, the police chief, had actually woken up much earlier than them because he had to attend to a very urgent warrant of arrest.

The laughter came to an abrupt end when the police chief walked in unexpectedly. He was shocked at what he saw, police officers holding their bellies in sudden silence after a dose of endless laughter.

'Have you executed the arrest warrant?' asked the police chief.

Laughter erupted again as the police officers enjoyed what apparently looked like the best joke ever created on April fools day.

'Shut up,' screamed the police chief to his officers. 'Have you executed the arrest warrant?' repeated the police chief with a seriousness that was last seen on his face when there was an attempted assassination of the President.

The police officers could not believe that their chief was taking the issue seriously. They were sure he must have had a lot to drink last night or had completely lost his mind.

'Sir,' quizzed one brave police officer, 'the warrant orders us to arrest Jesus Christ.'

'Yes it does and I ordered you to execute it,' rebuffed the police chief.

'But sir, Jesus is dead. He died twenty centuries ago, and that is almost two thousand years ago!'

'Officer Peter Saint Christos, are you a Christian?'

'Yes sir.'

'Is your Jesus dead or alive?'

'Alive sir.'

'Then get your a** out of here and arrest him.'

CHAPTER 2

Most Wanted

Huge billboards were erected in fifty two states of the United States of America. The image on all the billboards showed the features of what had now become the most wanted alleged criminal in human history.

Name: Jesus

Other names: Christ

Alias: Son of God, Saviour, Redeemer etc…etc

Ethnicity: Jew

Of medium height;

Last seen hanging on a cross in Jerusalem two thousand years ago;

Apparently escaped from a tomb.

Can be found trying to turn water into wine in drinking places.

Loves prostitutes, tax collectors, thieves and all others who go by the name sinners.

A reward of US$250 Million is offered for any information that may lead to his arrest.

It was difficult for the police to locate one of the most elusive persons the world had ever known. They wished Judas Iscariot was around. If thirty pieces of silver was enough for him, US$250 Million would make him kiss Jesus on both cheeks.

Surprisingly, the US$250 Million was claimed. Part of the deal was that the identity of the person who did give information that led to the arrest of Jesus be kept secret. The police kept their word. Jesus ended up Guantanamo Bay prisoner number 010010.

CHAPTER 3

THE APOCALYPSE

Thomas Doubt could not believe his eyes. He had it all, women, booze, drugs and God only knew what else. He held his mouth in disbelief. He could not believe that he had survived the end of the world. He looked again to see whether there was a great earthquake that he had not felt. He checked the Sun to see if it had become as black as the sackcloth, looked around for the moon that looked like blood and all he saw was a clear sky.

Thomas quickly looked below at the landscape to see whether the stars did fall to the earth, nothing and nothing at all. The sky had not vanished like a scroll that is rolled up as prophesied in the book of the Apocalypse and every mountain and island were still in their place. There was no burning in the fire and gnashing of teeth, as he had feared. He watched the television with a sigh of relief as he guzzled another mug of beer. 'I told these Christians that God did not exist and they did not believe me,' he said to himself. He laughed as he recalled how Christians quoted from their book of Apocalypse taunting him that he was going to hell. 'After all, why should I be burnt in eternal fire? All I did was enjoy myself. I never murdered anyone,' he consoled himself. 'And it is not a sin not to believe in God. It may be a sin to the Christians but not to God if God exists at all.'

This was meant to be heaven for Christians and hell for the rest. Paradoxically, it was now the Christians who were experiencing hell holding their mouths in disbelief as they watched Jesus being dragged in shackles to Guantanamo detention center. The second coming had certainly come like a thief in the night.

Little did Thomas know that he would end up being one of the twelve jurors who would decide whether Jesus was guilty or innocent? The summons came as a shock to him. He dutifully reported himself like nine hundred others who had to go through the gruesome jury selection process. Thomas doubted that any serious prosecution or defense team would even notice that he existed. He was wrong, whatever their reasons were, Thomas Doubt ended up juror number seven.

How was he, an atheist, to decide whether God existed or not? The answer was obvious. To Thomas Doubt, Jesus was just a figment of Christians' imagination. He made that very clear in the questionnaire that was handed to him in the jury selection process. He literally disclosed his verdict.

CHAPTER 4

URGENT LETTER

The phone rang and Iscariot Jones quickly answered it. The familiar voice of his secretary informed him of an urgent letter that was waiting for him. The last time he received such a call was when he was appointed as special prosecutor in a complex criminal trial involving top bankers that had embezzled millions of United States dollars from a bank in New York.

At fifty six years old Iscariot knew how to look after himself. He looked seventeen years younger. With a minimum of thirty minutes exercise every day and a strict diet that kept him away from junk food, his body was in good shape.

He has been a public prosecutor for thirty years, literally all his working life. Iscariot looked at his watch and knew that the morning traffic jam had eased. He got into his vehicle and drove straight to his office.

The envelope was written "urgent" in red ink. Iscariot opened it and could not believe his eyes. He was appointed as chief prosecutor in the trial of Jesus Christ. He immediately remembered Leonardo Da Vinci, the man who had been his mentor and inspiration in his career as a prosecutor.

Leonardo Da Vinci was a Scientist of enormous ability. He used his vast knowledge to deal with complex questions from science to arts and deserved to be among the best scientists that this world had ever produced.

What Iscariot Jones liked most about Leonardo was his ability to dissect. Something could look simple on the surface of it but Leonardo Da Vinci would dig deeper and get meanings that baffled inquisitive minds. He would dig to minute detail and express his complex findings in the simplest of ways. His painting of the last supper was a good example. Leonardo was intrigued with the life of Jesus but did not fall into the church brainwash of his time. He dug deeper and found amazing hidden truths about Jesus. Some truths were so complex that he had to be careful not to find himself in the same shoes as his fellow scientist Galilei Galileo.

Galileo was burnt on the stake by the Roman Catholic Church because of his scientific finding that it is the earth that goes around the sun and not the sun that goes around the earth. The writer of the Old Testament book of Joshua in the Bible was ignorant and made a wrong conclusion when he concluded it was the sun that moved around the earth. After all, he saw the sunrise and sun set.

This writer went on to put what he thought was the truth in the Bible and made God stop the sun in order to give the Israelites enough light to fight a battle. Galileo was therefore seen as challenging God when his finding was actually challenging the ignorance of the Biblical writer. The end result for him was death on the stake and the Catholics only apologized recently for wrongly burning him.

Iscariot too wanted to dig deeper. He wanted to dissect like Leonardo Da Vinci. He wanted to dig deep into Jesus and find all the hidden truths about him. In short, Iscariot simply wanted Jesus dissected "Da Vinci style".

CHAPTER 5

Strange Phone call

One hundred miles from Iscariot's office was Magdalene Royal. She too was in her office.

She was only twenty-nine years old, tall and beautiful. Being a Super model could have been an option but she chose to be a lawyer. Her beauty though attracted predator men who wanted to treat her as prey. Magdalene stood her ground and made it clear that she insisted on being treated as an equal.

She beat the men in her class but most of them got jobs before her simply because she was a woman. Law firms feared that unless a woman became like a man, she could not be a good lawyer. In other words, no getting pregnant, no children and no family, leave that family job to the wives of the hired male lawyers, they argue. And if you are a female attorney, too bad your husband cannot get pregnant; you will never have children.

Magdalene could not believe the chauvinist tendency of most law firms. They pretend to offer equal opportunities to both male and female job seekers. In fact, they even say preference would be given to the disadvantaged, especially women. This was just to cover up their As**s.

She however managed to get a job in a little known law firm and got the experience she wanted. With five years experience on her sleeves she set up her own practice in a little known area south of the city. Most of the cases she had dealt with were cases that did not attract any media attention. She hardly dealt with any criminal cases and spent most of her time on civil claims. Here she was, now sited in her own law firm wondering who her first client would be.

Her first work day at her law firm was one she expected to be quiet and uneventful. She had spent the previous day setting up her office she did not even know about the arrest of Jesus. She checked her telephone and confirmed that it was working. As soon as she put her receiver down it rang.

'Magdalene Royal Legal practitioners, can I help you?' she felt good finally saying her law firm name.

'Yes, this is the police chief. I have a very important detainee who wants to see you.'

'What is his name?'

'Believe it or not, Jesus Christ'

'There is nothing strange about that. Any person can give themselves an alias name Jesus Christ.'

'This is not an alias name, it is Jesus Christ.'

'You mean the detainee's actual names given to him at birth are the same names as those of the Jesus I worship at church?'

'No Miss Royal, this person is the Jesus you worship at church.'

'Is that what he is claiming, he should be delusional?'

'Not at all Miss Royal, he is as sane as you are and I repeat, it is Jesus Christ as in the one you worship. Are you the only one in town who has not heard about his arrest?'

The police Chief was right. Magdalene had missed the news and she still was not sure whether to believe him or not.

'Well, I will come and see for myself,' she finally concluded.

The first thing she did was checking the news. All radio and television networks were broadcasting the same news, the arrest of Jesus. What a beginning. Magdalene did not expect such a big client to kick-start her law firm. This was the kind of case that lawyers dreamt of. They would abandon their offices and sit in the whole trial in order to learn from top lawyers they expect to represent such big clients. But Magdalene was just an amateur. She was still very far from being called a QC or KC. Maybe one day she would be King's Counsel. KC!

But questions flooded her mind and she began to doubt. If it were really Jesus, why would he choose a little known lawyer from nowhere? This was a big case and it had already attracted so much media attention. Magdalene did not expect that she would be the one in the spotlight.

Fear engulfed her as she thought of the mockery that would follow if she made one simple mistake. The lawyers would be watching her every move, every word and every mistake she made.

CHAPTER 6

EASTER THROWN OUT

Jesus' lawyer made a preliminary application arguing that Jesus was already tried and sentenced two thousand years ago. She argued that trying him again was unlawful. Technical terms like "autre fois convict" were used to stress the point that it was not right for any human being to be tried twice for the same offence.

Iscariot, on the other hand, argued that the first trial was full of errors and should be set aside. In support of the application Iscariot went through what Christians were familiar with at Easter. A trial that started immediately after one of the worst tortures that a human being could receive; a trial that did not call any witnesses; and a trial that used a mob to make its final decision resulting in the conviction and execution of Jesus.

The Judge agreed with the prosecution and ordered that a fresh trial be conducted and that the prosecution were free to include charges that did not exist then but had become relevant due to new evidence against Jesus. Easter had effectively been thrown out and the Bible was damaged irretrievably.

CHAPTER 7

JESUS A FRAUDSTER AND A LIAR

The courtroom was called to order and the chief prosecutor, Iscariot Jones, stood up to give his opening address. He looked straight in the eyes of the jurors and gave them an address that sent shock waves across the world.

'This person that you see in the accused box ladies and gentlemen of the jury is the world's biggest fraudster, known by Christians as Jesus.

'The prosecution is going to show how, starting with his birth conspiracy, Jesus weaved a clever plan that included faking his resurrection to hood wink the unsuspecting followers into following him blindly. The prosecution will show how Jesus effectively used his so called autobiography, the Bible, to carry out his clever plan to brain wash more than two billion human beings better known as Christians. These people exist as I speak.

'Now Christians are forever marked with scars made by the torture and inhuman fear of a non-existent hell because of this man Jesus. Disguised as an angel of light, Jesus' evil plan will be exposed in this trial. Jesus will be dissected and shown to be a "man of the lie".

'The accused stands charged with four counts.

'The first is blasphemy. It is alleged that Jesus Christ claims to be God contrary to section one of Chapter one of the Deity Act which clearly states that no human being should claim to be God.

'The second count is a lesser charge of blasphemy that carries a sentence of life-imprisonment if found guilty. It is alleged that Jesus Christ claims to be Son of God contrary to section two of Chapter one of the Deity Act.

'The third count is treasonable conspiracy. It is alleged that Jesus conspired with known and unknown persons into black mailing and brain washing people to Christianity contrary to Chapter three of the Freedom of Religion Act. This man has brainwashed over two billion followers into submission to his multi-billion dollar empires that he intends to inherit.

'The fourth count is that Jesus has conspired to overthrow the world governments through his Christian empires. It is alleged that Jesus has conspired with known and unknown

Christian leaders to use his Christian empires to overthrow the world governments and become the world's leader.

'The prosecution will call a total of ten witnesses. Most of them will be expert witnesses for obvious reasons. We are dealing with events that happened two thousand years ago. It is impossible for the prosecution to bring the actual eyewitnesses. Luckily, we have experts who are able to use their knowledge and experience to help us see what really happened.

'The prosecution will start with two experts who will scrutinize Jesus' birth and show that what we celebrate on 25th December is just a fake pagan fable and a lie.

'The third witness will dissect Jesus' death and the so-called resurrection. This witness will prove that Jesus did not die on the cross and that the resurrection is just a cover up and has no truth to it.

'The fourth and fifth witnesses will show that, in fact, Jesus admitted the charges he is facing. He is therefore guilty from his own mouth.

'The sixth witness will show that Jesus had a secret wife, Mary Magdalene, and that Jesus' bloodline exists as I speak.

'The seventh witness will show that the Holy Grail is nothing but the womb of Mary Magdalene carrying Jesus' child.

'The eighth witness will show that Jesus is just a mortal man who was elevated to divinity at the Council of Nicea in 325 AD.

'The defense wants to use the letter G in their argument and the ninth witness will show that the letter G is an evil symbol used by the secretive society, the Freemasons.

'The last witness will be the complainant himself and his complaint is a matter of record.

'It will become clear as the witnesses testify that the Catholic Church knows these things and is hiding the truth.

'By the end of this trial, ladies and gentlemen of the jury, you will clearly see that Jesus is nothing but a criminal who deserves to die.'

He concluded by telling the Jurors that he expected only one thing from them, a guilty verdict.

CHAPTER 8

JOHN PUZIO

My name is Puzio, John Puzio. John was the name I was given at baptism when I was just a month old. I was too young to know what ritual I was being subjected to. After all, nobody seemed interested in asking me whether I wanted my head splashed with water inside some old building called a church.

I was therefore stuck with Jesus before I could even call my mother "Mum" and my father "Dad". I did everything expected of a good Christian boy; I shut my mouth and followed the rituals to the book. The priest called me a good and obedient boy.

My early years as a child were hard. I lost both my parents to the Aids pandemic. The stigma attached to such a disease made things worse. My friends and enemies alike looked at me as a living skeleton awaiting its death. They concluded that I did pick up the virus during birth. But it turned out that the loss of weight was simply from hunger.

I questioned this Jesus why he thought I did not deserve my mother and father. Little did I know that my questioning Jesus was the beginning of my relationship with him. When I read about how he suffered on the cross, I forgave him. He suffered enough, I thought.

My forgiving Jesus did not stop me from abandoning his church, its rituals, dogmas and doctrines. My eighteenth birthday was a celebration of independence from a church that had lost its meaning to me. Surprisingly, I abandoned everything except Jesus. I still felt that Jesus was with me even if I chose not to go to his church any more.

The news about Jesus' arrest was a blessing. The silence was over and Jesus would have to speak.

From Iscariot's opening address and the speculation of the newspapers, Jesus would have to tell the world whether he married Mary Magdalene and whether he had a child or children with her; whether the Merovingians who later became French Kings were his blood relations; whether he was just a mere man who was made divine by some narrow vote at the council of Nicaea in 325 AD. He would also have to tell the world whether the Catholic Church had been hiding the truth for almost two thousand years. There was no other way for Jesus but to explain his birth, death and resurrection.

In short, the world was waiting to hear from Jesus himself.

CHAPTER 9

FACT OR FICTION

I sat in court with mixed feelings. I did not know what to believe anymore. I was one of two billion Christians that had believed in Jesus and I sat watching my faith crumble right before my eyes. Was I so foolish to believe? Was I so blind not to see?

I looked at the prosecutor again and saw the certitude I had seen in his face when he finally declared to the jurors that they would find Jesus guilty.

For a second I told myself that this trial of Jesus was just a dream. The characters, places and events were either the product of someone's imagination or were used entirely fictitiously. This was fiction.

On second thought, it would be fiction if it were about a non-existent character. A dead person is never put on trial. If an accused person dies whilst undergoing trial the case abates; it comes to an end. This case therefore should have ended with Jesus' death almost two thousand years ago.

Tears welled in my eyes as I looked around the stadium courtroom. I looked again and realized this was no dream. This was no fiction. It was real. This man Jesus was undergoing trial almost two thousand years after his death because the dead man was alive. What we were dealing with was fact.

CHAPTER 10

THE DEATH OF CHRISTIANITY

Due to the magnitude of the trial, the whole world wanted to watch it live. Christians insisted they wanted to be present in the courtroom to give support to their leader. But which courtroom in the world would be able to hold a million people, let alone two billion? The compromise was to choose a stadium that could sit as many as possible and had the required security to hold such a trial. A decision was made to open up bids for any country that wanted to host the trial. The short listed bids were ten.

The Italians though put in the best bid. Their argument was simple. Thousands of Christians died in front of capacity crowds in Rome. There would be no better place for the trial of the man in whose name they died than the coliseum in Rome. Rome was the city that won the bid to hold the trial of the world's most controversial man, Jesus.

Jesus was extradited to Rome and a delicate jury selection process began. Twelve members of the jury were finally selected. A deliberate decision was made to ensure that the composition of the jury constituted six atheists and six Christians. Such balance would make it impossible for defense or prosecution to take advantage of a juror's belief or non-belief.

The prosecution had argued earlier that there should be no Christian juror on the jury because such a person would definitely be biased. The defense argued the opposite, that a non-Christian juror would definitely be biased. But Judge Manuel Curazon's ruling brought the dispute to an end with a clever insight into the meaning of bias.

'Bias means much more than being inclined to. It refers to an inability to serve as an impartial juror. I do not believe that simply because a Christian is inclined towards Jesus means that person will always support Jesus. Christians are known to abandon Jesus and I see nothing that would stop a Christian juror from making a decision against Jesus. The same with an atheist juror inclined against Jesus. We know of many atheists who have surprised their families and friends by suddenly becoming Christians. I rule therefore that even if all the jurors selected so far have specific inclination to or against Jesus this does not mean that they are biased. The job is on the prosecution and defense to persuade those not inclined to their arguments to change. This court will therefore proceed with a clearly divided jury with good reason,' the Judge had ruled.

Jury selection also took into account gender balance. The six Christians constituted three females and three males. The same thing was done to the six atheists.

In addition, the jury selection tried to cover the five continents of the world in order to give the trial an international presence because Jesus was an issue that concerned all five continents.

Iscariot was happy with the selection.

'I have six already on my side,' he thought to himself. *'All I have to do is convince three of these Christians that Jesus is a lie. This is a piece of cake.'*

His real target though was to convince all Christians to walk out on Jesus. After all they were vulnerable. They did not know what to think anymore. They thought they had four Gospels and they were shocked to hear the existence of more than thirty Gospels, which include, the Gospel according to Judas. In their confusion, Christians were looking for answers. The answer the prosecutor had in mind was that Christianity would be dead when the verdict was delivered. There would not be a single Christian in existence because more than two billion of them were going to abandon Jesus the same way he was abandoned on the cross.

CHAPTER 11

THE MYTH OF THE VIRGIN BIRTH

Every human being's story has a beginning. Jesus' story was no exception. Iscariot was eager to expose Jesus as a lie from inception. He innocently put a Bible in his brief case with suspicious intent. Law school taught him to begin trial with a strong witness. This would get the judge and the jury on his side and all he had to do was keep them on his side. There was no better way to start the trial than to call an expert in the field of conception. Iscariot was sure this was the witness to shatter the Christmas myth.

'I call upon the prosecution's first witness Professor Kimzinsky Telito,' declared Iscariot as he motioned his hand to the court clerk to usher in the witness.

The witness was sworn in and Iscariot began his questions in direct examination.

'What is your formal education witness?' asked Iscariot.

'I have an undergraduate degree, a medical degree and a doctorate degree.'

'Which undergraduate school did you attend?'

'Harvard University.'

'What degree did you obtain at Harvard University?

'A bachelor of Biology degree.'

'What was your major field of study?'

'Biology.'

'Which medical school did you attend?'

'Sorbonne medical school in France.'

'What did you obtain at Sorbonne?'

'My medical degree.'

'What did you do after graduating from medical school?'

'I interned at Victor Hugo medical center in Paris.'

'For how long?'

'Two years.'

'What did you do after those two years?'

'I became a resident.'

'What do you mean by resident?'

'I specialized in a specific field and got practical experience.'

'What field did you specialize in?'

'Conception and birth.'

'How long was your residence?

'Five years.'

'Where did you obtain your doctorate degree?'

'At Harvard University.'

'What was your doctoral thesis on?'

'The first nine months of a human being: Conception to birth.'

'Have you taught in the field of conception and birth?'

'Yes, I have lectured at several universities in United States and Europe.'

'Do you belong to any professional organizations?'

'I am the president of the Association of birth analysts.'

'Have you ever testified in a court of law on conception and birth?'

'Many times, specifically sixty times.'

Iscariot knew that he had adequately covered the formalities of an expert witness. It was now time to drop the bombshell.

CHAPTER 12

No Sense

I scariot proceeded with incisive questions on the merits of the case knowing exactly what his target was.

'As an expert on the genesis of human beings, can you tell this court the basic facts relating to the birth of a human being?'

'Every human being is born of the sperm of the male fused with the egg of the female,' said Kimzinsky Telito without ambiguity.

'The accused, Jesus, claims to have been born by divine pregnancy, does such a thing exist?' quizzed Iscariot as he turned his eyes with scorn to Jesus in the dock.

'No your honor, I repeat, a human being can only be born of the fusion of the sperm of the male and the egg of the female,' Telito re-emphasized his point.

There were shouts of "tell it all', "tell it all" across the stadium and the umpires were called to duty in the difficult task of keeping a stadium of two hundred thousand people quiet.

'What could have happened at the birth of Jesus?' Iscariot asked menacingly as he moved to the next segment of his argument.

'The sperm of Joseph and the egg of Mary formed the zygote Jesus nine months before Jesus' birth,' Telito answered clearly. He knew that a court of law was not the place to start using words with hidden meanings like "they knew each other".

The stadium court went dead silent. The little murmurs that were there earlier disappeared. Was this not blasphemy? If Jesus was not the Son of God were we not seeing the end of Christianity? As if this was not enough insult, the prosecutor proceeded with ease.

'Could there be a remote possibility that divine providence could have formed the zygote without any sperm? Iscariot inquired.

'Impossible. It actual makes no sense,' said Telito sarcastically knowing that he was just playing around with the words no and sense to say what he really wanted to say- nonsense.

Iscariot then took the Bible and put it as close to him as possible as if he was holding a weapon of war. He clenched his fist around the Bible with the fixed eyes of a sniper and advanced a step. His ring finger tapped on the Bible twice as he continued systematically asking his questions with precision.

'What does the accused say about his birth in his book called the Bible?' he asked as if the Bible was just one book.

'Objection your honor,' interjected Jesus' lawyer, 'the prosecutor's question is leading. It makes an assumption that the Bible is Jesus' book.'

'I am shocked that defense counsel is rejecting his own client's book,' Iscariot quickly replied as if he were the judge.

'Objection sustained. Proceed,' the Judge said as he ignored Iscariot's comment and ruled against the prosecution.

'I will rephrase my question. Do you know what the accused says about his birth?' quizzed Iscariot stubbornly.

'I know. It is clearly stated in his own book the Bible that he was born of some divine intervention,' parroted Telito, cleverly sneaking in the material objected to.

'Are you able to tell us the exact pages where his autobiography states his birth?'

'Yes, Matthew Chapter 1 verses 18 to 25.'

'Your honor, I ask for leave to hand to this witness a book.'

'Leave granted.'

It took less than a minute for the book to be passed on from the prosecutor to the witness. An evil smile crossed Iscariot's face as he watched with satisfaction his weapon of war rest in the witness' hand.

'Have a look at the book handed to you and tell this court what it is?'

'It is a Bible.'

'Can you read from the Bible Matthew 1 verse 18?'

'Yes, it reads and I quote, "This is how Jesus Christ was born. Mary his mother had been given to Joseph in marriage but before they lived together, she was found to be pregnant through the Holy Spirit" end of quote.'

'What is your opinion about that verse expert witness?'

'It is no sense,' said Telito, again playing with his favorite words.

'What do you mean witness?'

'As I indicated earlier, Jesus was born of the egg of Mary and the sperm of Joseph.'

'Are you saying there is no truth in this story?' Iscariot asked trying to sneak in his opinion.'

'Objection, the prosecutor is leading by inserting his opinion in the mouth of the witness,' screamed Magdalene, clearly alert to such tricks.

'Objection sustained,' the judge ruled in Magdalene's favor.

'Is the birth of Jesus stated anywhere else in the Bible?' Iscariot asked another question, this time acting like a gentleman – no tricks.

'Yes your honor, Luke Chapter 1 verses 26 to 38.'

'Can you briefly tell us in your own words what those verses claim?'

'That Mary was a virgin when she conceived.'

'What is your opinion on Mary conceiving as a virgin?

'No sense.'

'Are these two nonsense, pardon me, no sense stories similar?' Iscariot carried on knowing that he had deliberately used the word nonsense to give his witness' evidence weight.

'Surprisingly not, Jesus contradicts himself by telling us that he was born poor in a stable in the Gospel of Luke then changes to being born like a King in the Gospel of Matthew.'

'Any reason for the contradiction?'

'Only one reason, Jesus is not telling the truth.'

'No further questions.' Iscariot concluded and sat down.

CHAPTER 13

TELL IT ALL

There was silence as Iscariot sat down. How could the way, the truth and the light be said to be telling lies? All eyes moved to defense counsel. With a sigh of expectation, Magdalene Royal, Jesus' lawyer, stood up. She looked directly into the eyes of the witness and asked.

'Who wrote the book of Matthew?'

'Studies show that Matthew was written around 80 AD,' said Telito clearly dodging the question.

'Who wrote the book of Matthew?' Magdalene repeated her unanswered question.

'Earlier studies showed that it could be Levi, one of Jesus' apostles but the book was written after Levi's death. It is therefore not clear,' answered Telito knowing that he had not said it all.

'That was years after the death of Jesus,' Magdalene said as she changed her style from open to leading questions.

'Correct.'

'Going by your evidence, Jesus could not have written the Gospel of Matthew?'

'Correct.'

'When was the book of Luke written?' asked Magdalene as she went back to an open question knowing that the risk was minimal.

'In the year 70 AD'

'Was Jesus dead by then?'

'Yes, he was dead by 70 AD.'

'Who wrote the Gospel of Luke?

'A Syrian doctor who converted to Christianity'

'No further questions,' concluded Magdalene.

'Re-direct?' the judge asked looking at Iscariot.

'None your honor'

This was confusing. I could not believe Magdalene's line of questioning. Was she not supposed to be canvassing the assertion that Jesus inspired the Gospel writers and therefore wrote the books himself? Was she not supporting the prosecution by claiming that Jesus never wrote the Gospels of Luke and Matthew? This explained why Iscariot did not ask any questions in re-direct? How on earth could Magdalene be so blasphemous? Was there any hope for Jesus?

I knew that lawyers only argued according to their client's instructions. It baffled me to think that it was Jesus who gave blasphemous instructions to his lawyer. I sat there more confused than before as I anticipated the next witness.

CHAPTER 14

SHOCK IN THEIR EYES

Iscariot was happy with the damage caused by the first witness. He could see the disbelief in the Christians' eyes. Their pastors, parents and priests had kept this information away from them as if they were little children that could not swallow the bitter pill. The birth of Jesus was told every year in the midst of heavy spending, high booze sales and record church attendance to hear a story about some nice little baby born with an angel smiling in his face. Nice story but wake up and see reality, thought Iscariot.

He put his books in his large black box like shaped leather brief case and closed it. He then put his black court gown on his shoulder and left the stadium courtroom with his assistant Temazin Tallball. The two of them walked into the tunnel that led to their office and conference room. The office space was provided to the prosecution team to save them from having to drive to their usual offices at the Justice building, ten kilometers from the Coliseum. It would have been difficult for the two prosecutors to make it back in time after the terrible ever present traffic jam of the lunch hour.

'Did you see how one of those jurors looked at you Iscariot?' Temazin asked as he took a seat.

'I did and I could tell he wanted my blood'

'What made these Christians think the world would sit in ignorance and never question their Christmas story?'

'Ask their leaders. I am just doing my job and my job demands that the truth, the whole truth and nothing but the truth comes out.'

Iscariot smiled to himself as he relived the first witness' testimony. It was damage that had no recovery and could sympathize with Magdalene's difficulty in disputing the basic facts of life. His sinister motive, however, was not going to end here. He knew he could leave the conception and birth of Jesus issue to rest but he wanted another witness to come and consolidate the evidence of the first witness.

The six non-believers, on the other hand, seemed to have enjoyed the first witness. Their eyes brightened up as if the testimony was a justification of their unbelief. It was a pleasure for Iscariot to give them what they needed most, a justification. In that way, he could keep them on his side and keep pounding on the Christians.

CHAPTER 15

VATICAN CONCERN

The church bells rang in the emptiness of the sky. I was too far to hear them. There were coming from a small Romanesque church forty kilometers from the center of town. The priest in charge was an old gray haired man considered by the Vatican as having outlived his usefulness. His controversial theory of G-decoded almost earned him ex-communication. The final verdict however was to send him to a remote abandoned church. Only a few nuns from a nearby convent were his audience effectively reducing his public influence to zero. The Vatican had hoped that things would stay this way but they were wrong.

I left the stadium court when the trial was adjourned to the next day. I knew exactly where I was heading. What I had heard about G-decoded justified the forty kilometers trip to the small Romanesque church even if I had not been to church for many years. The tram ride was short and more comfortable than I had expected. I finally found myself entering the church.

I sat in the back row as I awaited the beginning of the service. The back row was always my favorite because it gave me a good view of all who were coming into the church. Better still, it was the best place for a quiet snooze if the preacher became dead boring. With so many big churches in the center of town, I could be the only visitor in this remote church, I thought. I was wrong. Jesus' lawyer walked in quietly and sat discreetly in the far right corner of a middle row. I was able to spot four members of the jury sited in different sections of the church.

The only reason why I was back at church attending a service was because I was interested in the rumor I heard about G-decoded.

The bell rang and the service began. I was not interested in the usual formalities of sit, stand, Kneel and sit. I reluctantly did them like a robot hardly waiting for the preaching time. Why didn't Catholics go straight into preaching than spend so much time on die-hard habits?

The Gospel passage had just been read, Matthew 1 verses 18 to 25. It suddenly dawned to me that this was the same passage that brought havoc in court. My tired dozing eyes suddenly awoke. Is this preacher going to use his G-decoded theory on this controversial passage?

CHAPTER 16

LOST IN NON-EXISTENT SPEECH

The priest moved away from his seat behind the altar and slowly walked closer to the people as he came to stand at the pulpit. Surprisingly, the church had filled to capacity at that time. It seemed people had heard about his famous G-decoded and they knew exactly what time to reach the church, sermon time.

'For those of you who are here for the first time, I welcome you to the church of G,' he spoke with an authoritative baritone voice.

I was not sure what he meant by G. Was this the abbreviation for God or the first sound of the name Jesus? As if reading my ignorance the preacher came to my rescue.

'For those who are here for the first time, G stands for Good and E stands for Evil. This is a church for good, G. After all the difference between Good and God is zero.'

Yes, he was right. If you subtract o from Good you remain with God and if you add zero to God you get Good. As I immersed myself in the mathematical fascination of the phrase, a deeper insight struck me. There was no difference. There was zero difference between Good and God. Yes, there was no difference, I exclaimed to myself as I continued listening to the preacher.

'When I was a priest at Sancta Maria mission in the remote district of Lukulu in Zambia, I heard so many African stories of how the hippo talked to the monkey and how the lion addressed a meeting of animals in the jungle,' continued the preacher. 'I never heard a single person ask whether lions talk. We all knew that the stories were simply vehicles of truth. It matters not whether a hippo can speak or whether a lion speaks English. Characters are necessary but free yourselves from the slavery of the characters of the story and you will see the truth.

'You ask yourselves', he reiterated, 'was Jesus born of the fusion of the sperm of Joseph and the egg of Mary? In short, was the father of Jesus Joseph or God? My brothers and sisters, you are lost in the non-existent speech of a lion. For as long as you keep wondering whether the lion spoke at all or whether the lion used English or French you will never know the truth. I repeat, free yourselves from the slavery of the characters of the story and you will see the truth. I wish you a fruitful week,' he ended.

CHAPTER 17

GIVE SOME MORE

Iscariot woke up early the next day and made sure the next witness was ready. Day one was gone and only one witness managed to testify. Iscariot hoped that more than one witness would testify on day two. The next witness was another expert on birth.

'The prosecution calls its second witness Professor Elizabeth Gisamo Macberth.' Iscariot announced.

Iscariot asked similar introductory questions as the previous witness but the answers were different.

'What is your formal education?'

'I have a masters degree and a doctorate degree.'

'Which graduate school did you attend?'

'University of Cambridge in the United Kingdom.'

'What degree did you obtain there?'

'A masters degree in history.'

'What was your major field of study?'

'The history of the Middle east.'

'Where did you obtain your doctorate degree?'

'At the University of Jerusalem in Israel.'

'What was your doctoral thesis on?'

'The history of Israel at Jesus' time.'

'Have you lectured?'

'I lecture at Oxford University and I give seminars and workshops to biblical scholars who want to understand the society in which Jesus lived.'

'Do you belong to any professional bodies?'

'Yes. I am the President of the Historians Association.'

'Have you ever testified in a court of law?'

'I have and it is usually in cases where the historical facts are in dispute.'

'How many times have you testified?'

'Sixty seven times.'

Iscariot was glad the formalities had come to an end. He knew lawyers had to be careful not to take too long on formalities least they lose the attention of the jurors. Iscariot was eager to get the most out of this witness. He took a deep breath and was ready to expose Jesus.

CHAPTER 18

Christmas Buried

'What does history tell us about how the cultures in which Jesus grew up reacted to matters of sex?' asked Iscariot.

'Jesus grew up in a male chauvinist anti sex society,' answered Professor Elizabeth Gisamo Macberth.

'Can you elaborate?'

'A woman was generally seen as unclean because of the male ignorance of the menstrual circles of their wives and daughters. Instead of seeing blood as a God given gift of life, blood from the menstrual circle was looked at with contempt.'

'Did that affect matters of sexual intercourse?'

'It certainly did. The male chauvinists thought sexual intercourse was a necessary evil that they had to undergo.'

'Is there any truth in these chauvinists' labels?'

'Not at all, Biology clearly teaches us and we all know from our own personal experiences that we are all creatures of excreta, both male and female and yet this has not made us unclean. We go to the toilet, discharge the unwanted excreta and continue with our lives clean. Having excreta in one's body does not make one unclean. We simply call it the call of nature…'

The stadium court erupted into laughter and shouted, "Give some more, give some more, Gisamo". Umpires did their job and the trial proceeded.

'Sorry for the interruption, you can proceed,' Iscariot motioned to the witness when he noticed that the witness still had more to say.

'It is surprising that males would look down on their female counterpart simply because of the menstrual discharge. The menstrual discharge is a God given call of nature which plays such an important role in the existence of human beings,' stressed Professor Gisamo.

'How did all this affect the conception and birth of Jesus?'

'It is easy to see. There was a conspiracy amongst the early Christians to suppress the truth by coming up with an impossible virgin conception.'

'And what is the truth that they were suppressing?'

'That Jesus was born through an act that resulted in the fusion of the sperm of Joseph and the egg of Mary to form the Zygote Jesus.'

'What is your opinion on arguments that Joseph was not Jesus' father?'

'If they mean God was the father, this makes no sense. But there is one possibility. Mary, the mother of Jesus could have been impregnated by another man.'

The crowd looked at the witness with shock.

CHAPTER 19

THE BOMBSHELL

Iscariot was excited with the bombshell that had shocked the crowd. He looked at the crowd to acknowledge their shock and moved on.

'Do we know who this other man who could have impregnated Mary was?'

'Tiberius Julius Abdes Pantera'

'Who was this Tiberius Pantera?'

'A Roman soldier'

'So Mary was busy playing around with Roman soldiers… she was some naughty girl…' insinuated Iscariot.

'Objection your honor, it is my client Jesus' character that is in issue and not his mother Mary,' complained Magdalene.

'I uphold the objection and advise the prosecution to avoid sensationalism,' ruled the Judge.

'My apology your honor,' intimated Iscariot. 'I will ask another question. Is Pantera mentioned in the Bible?'

'No.'

'Where then are you getting this information of Pantera?'

'It exists. The earliest record is from a Greek philosopher named Celsus who wrote around AD 178 that Mary was made pregnant by a Roman soldier.'

'Does this alternative story of the pregnancy of Mary contradict your expert opinion?'

'Not at all, my expert opinion is that there was sperm that came from a male human being that was fused with the egg of Mary. Whether that male was Joseph or Pantera makes no difference.'

There was applause in the stadium court and as soon as the Umpires did their job Iscariot pounced on the silence.

'I have no further questions,' concluded Iscariot.

'Cross examination?' asked the judge as he looked at Jesus' lawyer.

'No questions your honor,' said Magdalene.

I could not believe what she said. Did she say no questions? This was the most shocking thing that any lawyer could do. Fanatic Christians were now convinced that there was a conspiracy between the prosecution and Magdalene. How could she not cross-examine?

Media organizations had only one reaction- shock. Some concluded that because the witness seemed to be sympathetic to gender issues Jesus' lawyer, being a woman, had bought into the trick. She should have cross-examined the witness.

CHAPTER 20

KILLER BLOW

The second witness simply made things worse for Magdalene. When a lawyer decides not to cross-examine at all it could mean one of two things. Either the damage was so great that cross examination would simply make it worse or evidence supported a client so much that it was useless to question it. Iscariot concluded it was the first reason that made Magdalene shut up. According to Iscariot, he had unleashed the killer blow. He had finally shattered the beautiful unrealistic Christmas mythical story. The truth had finally come out.

'Do you think it is necessary to call another witness on the birth of Jesus?' asked Iscariot as he sat opposite his assistant in the prosecution conference room.

'Not at all,' replied Temazin Tallball.

'I thought so. Did you have a chance to gauge the reaction of the jury to the second witness?

'Yes I did. I believe the Christians are busy cursing their parents, priests and pastors for not telling them the truth about Christmas.'

'And the atheists?'

'No doubt they are smiling all the way.'

'I feel sorry for that beautiful Magdalene girl. She will lose this case with such shame and humiliation. Not a good foundation for starting a law firm.'

'She deserves the curse. She is such a stubborn feminist.'

'Well, enough for today. I look forward to the next witness. This one will be dynamite and will certainly finish off the already embattled Magdalene. He is testifying on death, which will certainly bring in Christianity's biggest death connection- the resurrection. I can't wait to show these Christians how fake their resurrection is,' concluded Iscariot as he called it a day.

CHAPTER 21

⊕PUS DEI INFILTRATI⊕N

Juror number one, Pierre Hugo, closed the door to his hotel room. It was a very expensive and exquisite suite. He was tired from the day's deliberations and wanted nothing but sleep. He looked at the King size bed waiting to grace his dreams. Hands that knew how to please a customer had spread purple linen fit for a King.

He looked around as if searching for something better than what he saw. He looked up in the huge wardrobe and saw exactly what he wanted. Up where his baggage was supposed to be starched away laid a detachable flat hard wooden piece. Pierre managed to remove it and put it nicely on the floor.

In this exquisite room that was the closest he could come to self-torture.

Pierre spent the next half hour inflicting pain on himself with a horse tail like whip. As if that was not enough, he tightened the barbed wired chain like belt called a cilice round his left thigh. It looked just like the crown of thorns on Jesus' head when you make a circle with it.

He reached for his traveling bag and got another cilice. This he tightened around his right thigh. With excruciating pain he lay on what he had now made his wooden bed eager to keep the cilices for more than the two hours maximum advised. After all, members of Opus Dei usually put one cilice and he had put two. Pierre was not going to disappoint Jesus the way his apostles did when they were advised to stay awake. He would endure the pain even in his sleep for he was ready for war against what he had seen as the scheme of the evil one to discredit Jesus. Blankets and bed sheets were ignored as he exposed himself to the cold of the night.

Pierre had not expected to end up juror number one. He had been in Opus Dei for twenty years. When the jury selection summons came to him he was away busy trying to recruit new members to what seemed to be the fastest growing Catholic organization in the world. Controversy aside, Opus Dei had done very well for a Catholic organization that was less than a century old. With assets close to three billion United States dollars and a thirty nine million dollar headquarters in New York, Pierre Hugo was convinced that Opus Dei had an inherent right to have at least one of them on what was now called the Jesus jury. They are not called die-hard for nothing. They are tough, resilient and committed. Was that not why Pope John Paul II made them his personal prelate?

The best representative the Catholic Church could have on the Jesus jury was an Opus Dei member and one of the most committed ones was Pierre Hugo.

To him suffering for Jesus was more than gold and he was more than ready to suffer and die for him. What Jesus was going through in the trial was to Pierre an insult to God. If he had it his way he would have asked Jesus to sleep in the hotel room and he Pierre would have taken Jesus' place in prison.

The usual conspiracies about Opus Dei made their rounds. There was a rumor that Opus Dei paid five million United States dollars to make sure that their member was one of the twelve jurors selected out of the nine hundred potential jurors. The fact that Pierre Hugo was selected first and called juror number one inflamed the suspicion about the five million United States dollars. This rumor was, however, short lived because no one could provide evidence of who was paid, when and how. It died just as a rumor but it scared the hell out of the prosecution that feared that if it were true then what would Opus Dei do next to make sure they got the verdict they wanted?

CHAPTER 22

THE JESUIT

The fear of Opus Dei was further compounded by the selection of a former Jesuit priest as one of the twelve jurors. Ignatius Brown was juror number two. He spent ten years as a Jesuit priest and left for what he called personal reasons. For the next ten years thereafter he continued to practice Ignatian spirituality, the spirituality the Jesuits follow, but now in a lay movement called the Christian Life Community.

His main attraction to Ignatian Spirituality was its founder, Ignatius of Loyola. A typical man of the world who dreamt of impressing beautiful women and being a famous knight, Ignatius of Loyola's dream was short lived in a battle where one of his legs was smashed with a canon. It was in his hospital bed that he finally encountered Jesus and later founded the Jesuits, a Catholic organization that dominated the Catholic Church for centuries till the coming of Opus Dei. The Jesuits were the most skeptical about Opus Dei and looked at its activities with suspicion. Suspicion has now settled into quiet rivalry as the two try to keep their influence on the Vatican. The two now find themselves sited next to each other in the names of juror number one and juror number two.

Former Jesuits are known to support Jesuits even when they were no longer part of the organization. To Pierre, Ignatius was not a former Jesuit but a representation of the Jesuits themselves.

The Jesuits' organization is called the Society of Jesus from which the initials S.J. come from. All Jesuits put the initials S.J. after their names. There is a joke that runs among Jesuits that Opus Dei and the Jesuits found themselves in a bitter fight involving the question whether God was Opus Dei or Jesuit. God got fed up with the unnecessary quarrel and wrote a letter to settle the dispute.

I am neither Jesuit nor Opus Dei. Signed God S.J.

CHAPTER 23

THE RIPPER

Dr. Jack Lipper was the first atheist juror to be selected. The numbers reserved for atheist jurors were seven to twelve and Lipper was juror number seven. He was an expert at dissecting. He surprised his parents when he was only eleven years old by giving them a detailed account of the inside of a rat. The parents could not find the book from which he could have read such detail. It was only when they went to the back yard that they found a rat cut into pieces. The lungs, intestines and stomach were put separately as if awaiting study.

'Did you do this son?' asked his father.

'I did.'

'Why?'

'I want to be a doctor.'

'Who told you that doctors go round cutting people?'

'Uncle is a doctor and I am told he is specialized in cutting people.'

'No, what your Uncle is specialized in is postmortems.'

'Post what?'

'Postmortems,' repeated the father, hoping that the big word would put off the inquisitive son.

'What is a postmortem dad?'

'My son, you ask too many questions, why do you not become a lawyer?'

'I am not interested in becoming a lawyer; I want to be a doctor.'

'But doctors spend most of their time using their hands whilst lawyers spend all their time using only their mouths.'

'Dad, what is a postmortem?'

'It is checking a dead body to see what caused its death.'

'How is the checking done?'

'Well, you cut a few sections of the body in order to see the inside of the body.'

'And if uncle wants to see inside the brain he cuts the head.'

'Yes, but …'

'That is exactly what I was doing dad, just like uncle.'

Jack Lipper did finally become a doctor and ended up specializing in dead human bodies. No one could cheat him about death. He too received a summons for the jury selection of the trial of Jesus. He was excited with it and he had only one reason why he really wanted to be on the jury. He had heard that the prosecutors had promised to dissect Jesus Da Vinci style. Who cared what they meant. If they were going to dissect Jesus, Dr. Jack Lipper had to be there.

CHAPTER 24

G

We all expected the trial to deal with more than one witness on day two. It ended up just like the first day – only one witness. The trial was even adjourned two hours before end of court hours. I took advantage of this and decided to visit the small Romanesque church again.

The church was closed since there was no service going on. Curiosity got me knocking on Fr. Perdo's door. It did not take long for him to open the door and he invited me in.

His house was a typical well-built Roman Catholics priests' house with very spacious rooms and a well-managed garden in the back yard.

After going to pains to make me feel at home, he finally asked if he could be of help to me.

'Yes, I am interested in knowing G,' I answered him enthusiastically.

'My God, are you serious?' asked Fr. Perdo looking surprised as if I had asked him for a million US dollars.

'Very serious,' I stressed.

'You mean you came all the way just for that?'

'I walked forty kilometers just for this.'

'I am impressed but you do not know what you are asking for.'

'I know, I want G.'

'God has a peculiar way of answering people's prayers, is it really your prayer that you want to know G?'

'You have asked me three times now and my answer is the same; teach me G,' I said wondering how many times he planned to ask me the question.

'Unfortunately, G is not taught the way we are taught in schools. If God wants you to know G, you will know G.'

I took advantage of his hospitality and asked him some questions. I told him about my concerns with the trial. I informed him that I was not following Jesus' lawyer's strategy. Maybe G could assist me understand. Fr. Perdo simply reminded me what he had said before that if God wanted me to know G, I would know G..

CHAPTER 25

ᛗURDER BY CRUCIFIXIⴲN

It was getting dark. I excused myself and went to take the tram ride. Father Perdo sat at his desk as soon as I was gone and started preparing a sermon. His residence was in one of the safest neighborhoods. Quiet and cut off from the evils of the big cities, this was the ideal place for sermon preparation.

A sudden chill filled the air. There was an unexpected bang that knocked open the front door. The man was swift to enter. Fr. Perdo tried to cool him down by offering him to take whatever material possessions he wanted.

'I am not interested in your material poverty. I am interested in something more important than that.'

'If it is something else that you seek then I am the wrong person to ask,' said Fr. Perdo.

'What you have been preaching clearly shows you know that which I seek. Tell me where I can find those that work with you,' demanded the attacker.

'Even if I knew I would not tell you young man,' said Fr. Perdo defiantly.

The attacker got infuriated.

'It seems you want me to do it the hard way,' said the attacker as he pointed the gun to the priest's head. 'Your death will be slow and painful and this will be a message to whoever is hiding what I seek that I will not hesitate to kill to get what I want.'

He tied the helpless old man with masking tape and laid him on the floor in cross-position. The priest could not move his legs because they were tied together. He could not say anything either because his mouth was covered with tape. His hands though were free and he wondered why his attacker left them like that. It did not take long for him to see the sinister motive behind the free hands. The attacker pulled one hand and got a huge nail and a big hammer.

'I guess you love Jesus. Well, let us see whether you are ready to suffer as he suffered.'

There was a big bang as the nail was hammered on the priest's wrist. A loud cry from Fr. Perdo got lost in masking tape. The attacker quickly held the other hand and did exactly what he had done to the first one. He then left the priest for a few minutes enjoying the pain of his victim as blood oozed out of the two injuries.

'That was what was done to Jesus in case you have forgotten,' taunted the attacker.

He then got a sword made of iron and struck it deep into Fr. Perdo's right rib. Blood guzzled out and the attacker continued talking.

'In case you do not read your Bible, Jesus was hammered with a sword on his right rib just like you. Now you know how he felt,' he paused. 'By the way, I almost forgot, Jesus' feet were nailed to the cross.'

He grabbed the other two nails he had and rammed them into the feet of Fr. Perdo. He laughed to himself and continued taunting.

'Fr. Perdo, did you think Jesus' death on the cross was a joke? Did you think that Jesus enjoyed being hung on that cross? You Christians claim you are his followers but have no idea how painful it was for poor Jesus to hung on the cross for you,' he muttered as he kicked Fr. Perdo several times on his chest.

The priest was now unconscious. The attacker on the other hand seemed to enjoy what he was doing.

'That is what we did to your Jesus. Enjoy it. By the way, if you think the pain you are undergoing is too much, keep in mind that Jesus was whipped severely before he got what I just gave you.'

The attacker then produced a whip and meted out six hard lashes on the back of Fr. Perdo.

'Poor Jesus, imagine the lashes I have given you are just a fraction of what your leader received,' he joked as he added two more lashes on Fr. Perdo.

Then the attacker seemed to run out of ideas. He opened his bag, took a Bible and quickly searched for the Gospels. He then picked on the Gospel according to Luke and went to the very end. He then flipped a few pages backwards till he saw the crucifixion title. He looked at the passage and smiled when he came across something he had not done yet.

'Oh yes, should I offer you a cup of tea or coffee? Well, I see you are thirsty; water would be a good idea.'

The attacker got a cup and put some water in it. He then removed the tape on Fr. Perdo's mouth who by now was almost dead.

'Drink Fr. Perdo, you are lucky that your death will be exactly like Jesus. You too can be a savior, a Son of God and maybe God,' he laughed as he tried to force the drink into the priest's mouth. He then shook his victim's body and noticed that it was lifeless.

'It is finished Fr. Perdo, it is finished. This is what you are supposed to be saying before dying,' screamed the man, visibly annoyed that the ordeal had ended too soon.

He pack all his instruments of torture and said his last words to the priest.

'I am not foolish Fr. Perdo. If I leave now, you could become conscious in three days. I will not be so foolish as to give you a chance to rise from the dead.'

He pulled out a pistol and shoot Fr Perdo twice on the forehead and thrice in his heart.

'Rise from the dead if you can,' he shouted as he banged the door and disappeared into the dark night.

CHAPTER 26

Cold Blooded Killer

The police arrived at the crime scene within five minutes after the murderer had fled. An anonymous call apparently from the murderer himself informed the police that a man had just been "Jesus crucified" in his house. The murderer gave the police the exact address where the body was. Police have had experience of such daring murderers who kill their victims and have the audacity to declare it to the police.

The whole house was cordoned and the police started the painstaking job of collecting evidence. Nothing was left to chance as forensic experts gathered every item that could possibly be a clue to the identity of the killer.

A mobile forensic lab was brought to the scene containing the most modern equipment in forensic science. When DNA was first introduced in 1985 a coin full of blood was needed to have any significant impact. But forensic science has advanced so much that a few cells smaller than a speck of dust can be used to identify the killer.

Items were collected from the house for forensic testing. Amongst those items was the cup that Puzio had used to drink his tea. His fingerprints were all over the cup. It was just a matter of time before the police identified whose fingerprints they were.

I could not stomach the news of Fr. Perdo's murder. I wondered why a human being would do such a thing. What had gone wrong for him to decide to take another person's life?

What good can exist in the murderer of Fr. Perdo? The cruelty with which the murderer carried out his crime made the little good that I could have seen in the killer disappear. I saw nothing but evil in him. How strange that Jesus was able to deal with such people.

If I knew the identity of the murderer I would have told the police immediately. If I had even just one clue or item that could assist the police I would have given them. But I am just as puzzled as everybody else wondering who would do such a bizarre ritual murder.

The murderer was clever enough to kill Fr. Perdo just minutes after I had left. The police would certainly put me as suspect number one if I told them that I was at the crime scene a few minutes before the crime was committed. With such a clever timing murderer on the loose I might spend months in cells before someone finally declared me innocent. The trial of Jesus would by then be finished.

CHAPTER 27

Finito Pinto

Day three looked promising. Iscariot was sure he would deal with more than one witness this time.

Juror number seven, Dr. Jack Lipper, looked keenly at the third prosecution witness. Iscariot had introduced him as an expert on death. This certainly caught the attention of Lipper because most dissections he knew were done on dead bodies. It was an area he knew very well. He was interested in how the witness was going to deal with the death of Jesus.

The witness was sworn in and Iscariot proceeded.

'What is your name witness?'

'Dr. Finito Pinto.'

'What are your formal qualifications?'

'I have a masters degree and a doctorate degree.'

'Which graduate school did you attend?'

'University of Hummington.'

'What graduate degree did you obtain?'

'A masters degree on death.'

'What was your major field of study?'

'Murder.'

'Where did you obtain your doctoral degree?'

'At University of Strangulant.'

'What was your thesis on?'

'Suspicious death.'

'Where did you carry out your doctorate research?'

'In the middle east.'

'Any example of suspicious deaths you investigated?'

'Yes, the suspicious death of Jesus the Christ.'

'Thank you witness; let us now move to the merits of this case,' concluded Iscariot as he moved to the main part.

CHAPTER 28

DEATH OF RESURRECTION

'What is death witness?' asked Iscariot.

'Death is a cessation of life,' answered Dr. Finito Pinto.

'Do you know anything about the accused Jesus' death?'

'Yes I do. Jesus died in AD 64.'

There were clear murmurs in the stadium court as everyone thought the witness had made a mistake. Who did not know that Jesus died in his thirties? This was just a slip of the tongue.

'When does his religion say he died?' continued the prosecutor.

'AD 33.'

'By death you mean what?'

'As I earlier indicated, it is a cessation of life?'

'Can you explain the meaning of a cessation of life?'

'By that I mean Jesus' flesh got rotten into dust and what remained was just a skeleton- Finito.'

The stadium court burst into laughter. The crowd shouted, "Finito, finito, finito". Umpires got to work and silence followed.

'What makes you so sure that it happened in AD 64 and not AD 33?' continued Iscariot.

'Jesus appeared to people after his so called death in AD33 but never appeared to anyone after his actual death in AD 64,' answered Finito Pinto.

'Any examples of his appearances?'

'Yes. He appeared first to Mary Magdalene and then to his apostles.'

'Any reason why he never appeared after AD 64.'

'He was dead, reduced to a skeleton, never to be seen alive again.'

'Are you able to explain why we have ended up with conflicting dates of the death of Jesus?'

'Yes I can. Jesus did not die on the cross in AD 33. He was crucified on the cross but that was part of his plan to fake his death and create a resurrection. This he did successfully and he finally died in AD 64 in Rome.'

'Can you say more about what you mean by fake his death?'

'There was a conspiracy between Jesus and his apostles to cover up his death. Judas Iscariot, unlike common belief, was actually the right hand man who knew the plan in detail and played a big role in executing it.'

'Where are you getting all this information about Judas?'

'In the gospel according to Judas.'

'Did you say the gospel according to Judas?' asked Iscariot pretending not to have clearly heard the answer.

'Yes I did.'

'Is it one of the Gospels in the Bible?'

'No.'

'Any reason why not?'

'The gospel of Judas was discarded by the early Christian church in order to hide the conspiracy between Jesus and Judas.'

'By early Christian church you mean who exactly?'

'Bishop Ireneaus branded the Gospel of Judas heresy.'

'When was this?'

'In 180 AD.'

'Any reason given for the heresy brand?'

'In the Gospel of Judas, the one who really knew Jesus was Judas Iscariot and Judas is portrayed as Jesus' closest ally. This was branded heresy because the four Gospels chosen portray Judas as a thief influenced by Satan.'

'Do we have any copies of the Gospel of Judas today?'

'Fortunately yes. Even though the Gospel of Judas was destroyed a copy survived and was discovered.'

'In what form was it found?'

'It was in leather bound book called a codex and was written in Coptic.'

'How far back did the copy that was found date?'

'Carbon dating put it at 280 AD plus or minus fifty years.'

'Your opinion witness?'

'Jesus' death on the cross was fake.'

'No further questions.'

CHAPTER 29

ᛗAGDALENE FIGHTS BACK

Magdalene knew that the witness just touched the greatest controversy of history. She knew the kind of questions the jurors would be entertaining. Did Jesus really rise from the dead? Are we not simply dealing with a major cover up? Is this not the biggest scandal and conspiracy of all times?

Magdalene stood up and placed herself in a position where she could have good eye contact with the witness.

'You are an expert on death, correct?'

'Correct.'

'An expert on death after life?'

'Correct.'

'But you are not an expert on life after death, are you?'

'I am an expert on all kinds of death.'

'How many kinds of death do you know?'

'Only one.'

'Which one.'

'The one where your flesh rots and you are reduced to dust leaving only your skeleton.'

'By that you mean death that comes after someone is born?'

'Correct.'

'What about life that comes after death?'

'There is no such life.'

'Why do you say there is no such life?' asked Magdalene defying advice in law practice that says avoid why questions because you give the witness a chance to explain.

'We see dead bodies every day and we find only skeletons if we ever check the graves. No record of a human being living after death.'

'So your determination that Jesus died in AD 64 and not in AD 33 is based on a record of appearances around AD33 and no record of similar appearances around AD 64.'

'Correct.'

'Are we not in the twenty first century?'

'We are.'

'Is the twenty first century not after what you call the death of Jesus in AD 64?'

'It is.'

'Can you see Jesus in the stadium court today?'

'Yes, I can. He is seated in the accused box.'

'So Jesus has appeared after AD 64?'

'Umhmmhh... yhx*x*... I suppose yes. You are right,' confirmed the witness, looking stunned and clearly baffled.

'No further questions.'

Jesus' presence was a problem to Iscariot. He would not even dare challenge it. The whole trial was based on the fact that Jesus is alive today. If he were not alive, the police would not have arrested him. The best way out was not to ask any questions at all to this witness in redirect and that was exactly what Iscariot did.

CHAPTER 30

Doctor Adminton Admita

The fourth prosecution witness was one that every lawyer would fear, a confession expert. What better way to find an accused guilty than through their confession?

Iscariot walked into the courtroom stadium from lunch with confidence oozing all over his face. Day three had lived to its promise. A second witness was coming to testify on the same day.

He was happy with what he had done so far even though he could not re-examine the previous witness. The next witness, however, had Iscariot all excited. There was no better weapon in criminal trials than a confession of the accused. Who did not know that a confession was the unequivocal admission of guilt? Evidence before court showing that Jesus admitted his own guilt would be devastating to the defense.

Several experts on confessions were contacted. Dr Adminton Admita was the one that Iscariot finally settled for. What he liked most about this witness was not so much the knowledge of confessions that he certainly had but the sarcasm with which he presented his evidence. Iscariot wanted the thrill of seeing Magdalene fidget, twitch and tears of defeat well in her eyes.

'What is your full name witness?'

'Dr Adminton Admita.'

'Your formal qualifications.'

'I have a Masters degree and a doctorate degree.'

'What did you specialize in when doing your Masters degree?'

'Criminology.'

'And your doctorate?'

'My doctorate dissertation was on confessions.'

'Any experience in the field of confessions?'

'Yes, I was specially trained to hear confessions in the Catholic Church when I was a priest. For five years I was tasked with the responsibility of hearing the Pope's confessions.'

'Have you testified before on confessions?'

'Not at all.'

'Any reason why not?'

'I swore not to reveal the confessions I have heard especially the Pope's.'

'Why are you here then?'

'To testify on a confession I never dealt with.'

'Whose confession?'

'Jesus.'

CHAPTER 31

Jesus' Criminal Confession

I scariot was interested in Jesus' confession, not the Pope's.
But he wanted to make sure that everybody in the stadium
court knew what a confession was.

'Witness, what is a confession?' Iscariot started examining
the fourth prosecution witness in chief.

'It is an unequivocal admission of guilt.'

'What do you mean by that?'

'By that I mean a person saying something that amounts to
admitting the elements of the crime he is charged with.'

'Are you aware of any confession by the accused Jesus?'

'Yes, I am.'

'Is it verbal or written?'

'Written.'

'Where is it written?'

'Mathew Chapter 16 verses 13 to 23.'

'What do those verses say?'

'That the accused asked his disciples who they said he was.'

'Was there any answer?'

'Yes, Simon Peter replied saying that Jesus was the Christ, the Son of God.'

'Any reaction to what Peter said by Jesus?'

'Yes there is. Jesus told Peter in verse 17 of the same Chapter that and I quote, "Blessed are you Simon Barjona! For flesh and blood has not revealed this to you, but my father who is in heaven.'

'Expert, tell us what this scripture jargon means?'

'It is easy to understand. Peter claimed that Jesus was the Son of God and Jesus agreed with him saying such answer could only come from God. This is a clear confession and it amounts to Jesus admitting the criminal charge he is facing.'

'No further questions.'

CHAPTER 32

DEAD END

Magdalene had to be careful. Iscariot had pushed her into a corner. Admit the confession and Iscariot would have proved the charge that Jesus claims to be the Son of God, and if she denies it she would be proving that Jesus was fake and a fraudster.

'Look at exhibit one, the Bible and go to the Gospel of Mark,' instructed Magdalene.

The witness quickly flipped the pages and looked back at Magdalene with a menacing stare.

'Look at Mark Chapter 8 verse 2 and following. Is that not the same story as the one you call a confession in the gospels of Luke and Mathew?'

'Yes it is,' admitted Adminta.

'Except that it is different from the one in Luke and Mathew.'

'Correct.'

'What is the difference?'

'Mark is the shortest and does not include a confession on Son of God.'

'Of the three Gospels, which one is the earliest?'

'Mark.'

'Is it correct that the writers of Luke and Mathew had Mark when writing their Gospels?'

'Correct.'

'So the writer of Mathew had Jesus' answer in the gospel of Mark.'

'Correct.'

'Which is that Jesus was the messiah.'

'Correct.'

'If you compare what the writer of Mathew had from Mark and what was finally written by him, what explanation have you got for the difference?'

'The writer of Matthew added on to what the writer of Mark wrote.'

'Why?'

'Because there was then a belief by early Christians that Jesus was the Son of God.'

'So what did the writer of Mathew do exactly?'

'He took what was written in the Gospel of Mark and added on the new belief.'

'And what year was the gospel of Mathew written?'

'Around 80 AD.'

'Way after the death of Jesus.'

'Correct.'

'And what happened to the Gospel according to Luke?'

'The writer of the Gospel of Luke did to Mark exactly what the writer of Mathew did to Mark.'

'What do you mean?'

'Luke added on the early Christians' belief to what he found in Mark.'

'Which year was that?'

'Around 70 AD.'

'Is what is written in Mark pertaining to the same story a confession by Jesus or not.'

'Actually not, the criminal confession by Jesus does not exist in the gospel of Mark.'

'No further questions.'

CHAPTER 33

WOUNDED BUFFALO

This time Iscariot admitted defeat on the confession attempt. Dr. Adminton Adminta did not work out as planned. Magdalene had clearly cast doubt on the apparent additions made to the Gospel of Mark by the writers of the Gospels of Luke and Matthew. This, however, did not deter Iscariot from trying Plan B. He had learnt, during his thirty years as prosecutor, to always have plan B. He had another witness to testify to another confession by Jesus which Iscariot was sure had no escape route for Magdalene. Iscariot could smell victory from the chains of recent defeat.

'Your name witness?' asked Iscariot.

'Dr. Konfesio Londington.'

'Your qualifications?'

'There are indicated already in the documents on record. I am not sure whether it is necessary for me to bore the court with an hour of qualifications citations.'

'It is not necessary for you to repeat that. I already have record of your qualifications,' jumped in the Judge.

'Your experience?'

'That too is already on record. It may assist you to know that I am the one who supervised Dr. Adminton Adminta's doctorate dissertation.'

'Do you know of any confession by the accused Jesus?'

'Yes I do.'

'Written or verbal?'

'Written.'

'Where is it written?'

'In the Gospel of Matthew Chapter 26 verses 63 to 65.'

'Can you tell us what happened?'

'Jesus is asked a question whether he was the Son of God?'

'Any answer from Jesus?'

'Yes.'

'What was the answer?'

'You say so.'

'Tell us the reaction of the person who questioned Jesus after he heard Jesus' answer?'

'I quote verse 65 of the same Chapter, "Then the high priest tore his robes and said, 'he has uttered blasphemy. Why do we still need witnesses? You have now heard his blasphemy." End of quote.'

'What is your opinion expert witness?'

'This was a clear confession.'

'What do you mean by clear confession?'

'Jesus unequivocally admitted he is the Son of God which amounts to admitting the elements of the crime of blasphemy.'

'What gathering was this?'

'It was before the Sanhedrin.'

'What was a Sanhedrin?'

'The equivalent of a court of law.'

'And who was the high priest in the Sanhedrin?'

'The equivalent of a judge.'

'In other words Jesus made his confession before a Judge in a court of law.'

'Correct.'

'And we have his confession in writing in exhibit 1, the Bible?'

'Correct'

'No further questions.'

CHAPTER 34

JESUS CORNERED

Magdalene knew that the fifth witness was harder than the first confession witness. She knew she was back in the same problem she faced earlier. If she agreed that Jesus was Son of God that would be admission of guilt. If she did not agree, Jesus would then be considered fake and a fraudster. She decided to make her questions short and to the point.

'You quoted Jesus as saying "you say so", what is the meaning of "you say so"?

'It means you are the one saying so,' answered Dr. Konfessio.

'So according to Jesus it is the accusers who claim he was the Son of God.'

'Yes, that would be the literal meaning of 'you say so''

Then Magdalene made a sudden twist.

'Your name is Dr. Konfessio Londington,' she asked cautiously.

'Yes, it is.'

'Is your answer a confession or not?'

'I am just stating what I am.'

'Is there anything wrong with stating what you are?'

'Not at all.'

'Let us assume Jesus is actually Son of God, would it be wrong for him to confess what he is?'

'Not at all.'

'No further questions.'

What? My God, did Magdalene just admit that Jesus did claim to be Son of God? Did she really know what she had done? She had literally shifted the burden to Jesus to prove to the jurors that he was Son of God and how was she going to do this? Jesus Christ, what a gift!

Iscariot could not believe his luck. Magdalene had started off well with her "you say so" argument but messed it up with name argument. He was defeated just an hour ago but here he was enjoying the sweet taste of victory.

CHAPTER 35

GIGANTIC FRAUD

'*Hard hitting prosecutor, stubborn defense lawyer and a bit of sarcasm in between, this is just like a Hollywood block buster script!*' thought Juror number seven, Shaka Chaka. He was enjoying every step of the trial. He did not expect it to be as dramatic as it was. But there was something that was troubling him. How did he end up as an atheist juror?

He was one of few Africans that made it to the Juror selection process and ended up the only African selected on the Jesus jury. He had no problem at all with that but he thought he would find himself in the other half of the jurors called believers. He remembered clearly giving a big NO to a question whether he was a Christian. But it seemed nobody was bothered about what he believed in. As soon as he said he was not a Christian questions followed on whether he was Muslim, Buddhist or Hindu. He refused to answer the questions because he considered them leading. *Why not ask me what I believe as opposed to imposing the religion you want on me*, he remembered asking. Iscariot was impressed that Chaka could distinguish a leading question from an open one. He liked him and wanted him on the jury. In the end Chaka was selected as an atheist juror.

The problem he had with being called an atheist was that he actually believed in God. But the name of the God he believed in did not make a hit on the World Wide Web.

Chaka felt unfairly treated. This was exactly what happened to his forefathers and mothers. They were called pagan yet they were all believers and had a name for God.

Most of his relatives and friends were now Christians. What this meant to them was something Chaka was yet to understand. They say they had changed, abandoned their evil practices and were baptized in the spirit. But Chaka still saw them committing evil. The Minister of Home Affairs had just asked for funds to expand the prison cells because crime was growing at an alarming rate. Every one of those convicted sign Christian under religion. Chaka did not understand why Christians committed evil. *Was it because their savior Jesus was weak? Has the evil one more power than Jesus?* He wondered.

He was excited when he was called for jury selection. He was going to see with his eyes this Jesus who had caused a lot of damage to his home town. His churches were full of people praising and singing his name leaving Chaka and a few die-hard traditionalists still worshipping God up a mountain.

Chaka experienced his biggest horror when almost eight hundred thousand Tutsi and moderate Hutus were massacred in the Rwanda genocide. He recalled being in that country at that time working as a volunteer. The same people who filled the churches singing praises to Jesus abandoned their Bibles and massacred others with machetes, spears and knives. The same Christian churches were turned into massacre chambers.

Chaka survived twice. Once when a machete wielding ferocious man held his throat and asked him whether he was Tutsi. Chaka had cried in his mother tongue and that was how the attacker spared his life when he was convinced that the cry he heard was a foreign one.

The second time was simply by the grace of God. He took shelter in a big church hall with many others when the attackers came and started butchering people like cows. Chaka was one of only five who survived simply because there were too many bodies lying on the floor and the attackers could no longer distinguish who was dead and who was alive especially if you lay still.

From that time Chaka cursed the Christian religion for bringing such misery. Jesus failed to stop the massacre. Jesus was powerless to the evil one. Christianity had failed to change the person from the inside.

Chaka still wanted to know why Christians did evil. *Were they not just Sunday Christians who spent the others days of their week serving their real master, the devil.*

Chaka hoped the trial of Jesus would answer his questions. Africa would be waiting to hear for itself whether this religion called Christianity was truly from God or just one gigantic fraud.

CHAPTER 36

UNFAIRLY TREATED

Namasaki Kamamoto sat expressionless next to Shaka Chaka. She was from Japan. She too was chosen as an atheist juror. Chaka believed that what had happened to him was exactly what had happened to Namasaki. Chaka himself had never heard of the religion that she believed in and it was no wonder she was sitting as an atheist juror.

Another victim of the same treatment was the lady from China. She too was unfairly categorized as an atheist. She could not understand why Christians felt their way was the right way. She came from a country with over one billion people. She knew a lot of good Chinese people who were not Christian at all. Questions kept ringing in her mind.

Why would Christians want to throw their hell fire on non-Christian Chinese? Why does their God enjoy torture of a human being in endless fire? Why are Christians wasting time and energy trying to convert the Chinese? China already knows God and good. Christianity did not have monopoly to good. Other religions too have God.

CHAPTER 37

Target the Jury

Iscariot called an urgent meeting with his Assistant. He wanted to know what was really happening to the jurors.

Four witnesses had testified so far. Iscariot felt it was time to try and read the mind of the jurors. The ones he was more interested in were the Christian jurors; numbers one to six.

Temazin took out a list of the twelve jurors and passed it to Iscariot. He then reached for his big brief case and removed a camera. It was small but good enough to take clear pictures of the jurors in court.

The two of them then looked at the reaction of the Christian jurors during and after each witness' testimony. Iscariot looked at his list of Christian jurors. Pierre Hugo, Ignatius Brown, Maria Spirit, Sabaday Kingston, Whitney Queenston and Hildergate Luther.

According to Iscariot, the toughest one to crack would be the Opus Dei juror who seemed to be supporting Jesus no matter what. The other tough one was Maria Spirit. She was lost in the spirit and this might make it tough for Iscariot to win her over.

The easiest to win over was Whitney Queenston. As a Watchtower, she did not believe that Jesus was God. This made it easy for Iscariot to convince her.

Ignatius Brown was a thinker and used his head to make decisions. This made him the next easiest target. All that was needed was the clever use of knowledge to convince him.

Sabaday Kingston was another easy one. Her pillar was only the Sabbath. Destroy that and she falls.

That made three already that could be won over. You add the three to the six atheists and Iscariot wins the case. Jesus loses.

CHAPTER 38

Jurors' Confusion

Whilst Iscariot was busy guessing about the jurors, what was happening in the jury room was something that not even Iscariot could have guessed. It was a scene that usually attracted media attention in football matches for wrong reasons; two sides trying their best to win a game and the referee trying his best to keep the peace only to be spoilt by a sudden Zidane head butt.

The head butt came from Pierre straight into the rib cage of Thomas Doubt. The Christians rushed to restrain Pierre and the atheists did the same with Thomas before things could get worse. It was not clear what Thomas had done which made Pierre so angry. Whatever it was should have had something to do with the fact that one was a Christian and the other was an atheist. It was clear that jurors were divided into two camps as was expected. To keep the peace, the two camps agreed to disagree.

There was peace for a while as each one of the jurors pondered what had just happened. It was clear that even when taking their tea and coffee break, each camp stood in their own corner. That created a buffer zone to avoid another head butt.

Surprisingly, there was another sound of a head butt. Every juror looked to the other camp to see what had happened. Only Pierre and Ignatius never bothered to look because they knew exactly who butted whom. Ignatius had butted Pierre for reasons only known to himself. Pierre charged at Ignatius to revenge the head butt he just received and he pushed his neatly shaven head deep into the chest of Ignatius.

'Is this all you can do, you son of a something? Ignatius retorted as he flung a second head butt into Pierre.

Both Christians and non-Christians rushed to restrain the two. To Thomas, this was the moment of truth.

'Tell me Pierre,' Thomas jumped in, 'I thought that head butt came my way because I was an atheist. Tell me why you head butted your fellow Christian? Has Jesus failed to unite you?'

'Mind your own business,' answered Pierre.

'I will not shut up Pierre. I am serious. Why are you Christians head butting each other?'

'Listen Thomas, you are an atheist. You can never understand the things of God. Heaven to you is just a figment of someone's imagination.'

'But I know what a head butt is. I received one from you a short while ago.'

'Listen Thomas,' joined in Ignatius, 'Pierre has told you to mind your own business.'

'Oh, now you have become friends again because you see me as your common enemy? Why do you not simply answer my question? I want to know why you head butted each other?'

CHAPTER 39

More Confusion

It seemed the time was ripe for neutral intervention. Lipper tried to diffuse the situation.

'It seems the separation into Christian and non-Christian camps have not worked at all. Head butts will continue unless we find something to unite us,' advised Lipper. 'Some key maybe… some lost wisdom or a miracle.'

'But there can be nothing between us and atheists unless you, Thomas Doubt and your fellow non-believers confess your sins, repent and accept Jesus as your personal savior,' hissed the evangelical juror Maria Spirit.

'Keep your Jesus to yourself. I am not interested in a Jesus who head butts,' Thomas reacted.

'How can you say that about my Lord and savior?' shouted Spirit as she approached Thomas angrily.

'Anhaaa.. You want to head butt me too. Go ahead and do it,' dared Thomas as he put his hands up to tempt Spirit.

And that is exactly what Maria Spirit did. She sunk her head deep into Thomas' stomach. It was too hard and too painful from what he had expected.

'That will teach you never to insult my Lord,' stressed Spirit.

Thomas was shocked as he held his stomach in pain gasping for breath. He could not believe that she actually did it. And her head is as hard as a rock. The first thing that came to his mind was revenge but he restrained himself.

'Is it not strange,' jumped in the quiet juror Hildagate Luther, 'that Thomas had the strength to restrain himself and we, the followers of Jesus, are failing to do that. Does this not tell us something about ourselves?'

'Oh my God, now we have a Christian who has just lost her faith and is supporting an atheist,' Ignatius cut her short.

'No Ignatius, you think too much, why do we not start by treating each other as human beings? Were we not all created in God's image? I think we are all capable of good,' said Hildergate softly.

'I am not going to succumb to the flesh. Now you want to elevate non-believers to believers? This is bull shit,' lambasted Ignatius.

'But you did succumb to your flesh. You head butted Pierre,' Hildergate reminded Ignatius.

'Well, he asked for it,' slashed Ignatius.

'So stop treating each other like animals,' Hildergate tried to cool him down.

'I agree with the quiet one. It is time we treated each other like human beings,' interrupted Shaka Chaka.

'What is this nonsense?' jumped in Maria Spirit again. 'It seems we are diluting our Christianity by accepting atheists.'

The squabbles continued with no end in sight till the jurors were summoned for the afternoon court session. The jurors walked to their seats wondering what the hell happened. Only the words of Lipper kept ringing in their ears. The key-the key-the key.

CHAPTER 39

Mysterious Man

I woke up late that morning. I took a quick shower, almost upset my stomach with the speed at which I threw food into my mouth and left my apartment quickly. Day four of the trial promised to be tough.

As I turned a corner I saw a man 500 meters away who seemed to be in pain. I could see clearly one well dressed man literary pass under the nose of the injured man without even looking at him. Then I saw a second man dressed in a cassock approaching the man in pain. I was now near enough to see that the man in pain was badly injured and needed help. I slowed down in order to give the holy priest a chance to do what he must. To my shock the priest simply crossed the road and continued walking as if he were the only person present.

My turn was approaching fast. As I got one step closer I noticed the injured man was a beggar who seemed to have been beaten up, possibly during the night. He was full of bruises with blood clearly showing.

Well soon some policeman will pass by and help this man. I am too much in a hurry. I argued with myself.

The beggar called out to me the same way he had done with the two I saw. His face looked half dead. It dawned to me that the two who decided not to help could be rushing for the same thing I was rushing for. After all, two hundred thousand of us got up every morning for the rush to the Coliseum. One needed to be nuts in the head to miss a minute of the trial of Jesus for a beggar.

Compassion, however, got the better of me. I came back to my senses and decided to at least offer some water to the beggar. I reached for the smallest of the five water bottles I was carrying and knelt to give it to the beggar. He looked into my eyes and said something that shocked me and would change my whole life.

'Thank you Puzio, I knew you would stop.'

How did this beggar know my name? Who is he and why was he beaten up?

'You may be wondering how I got your name. I got it from Father Perdo,' he continued.

'The priest who was murdered?' I inquired.

'Yes.'

'Why would he give you my name?'

'It is a long story. Go on to the trial and I will come and get you from your apartment at six in the evening.'

'You know where I live?'

'Do not worry about that. Just be at home by six.'

CHAPTER 40

BLOODLINE EXPOSED

I had a sleepless night and could not concentrate on the trial that morning. My mind was still with the beggar in the street. Why did Father Perdo give him my name? And why does he want to see me?

Excitement turned to fear when I recalled what the beggar had done. This could be some undercover agent investigating the murder of Father Perdo. The six p.m. appointment could be an arrest warrant for me. If this man knew that I visited Father Perdo just before he was murdered, the police may have been informed. Yes, I did visit the murdered priest several times just before his death but I have no clue who murdered him and why.

My thoughts were interrupted by the court clerk who called the next witness. The witness was one whom Magdalene had difficulty dealing with. His name was Nworb Nab, nick named in academic circles as "NN". NN had done the most extensive research on the bloodline of Jesus and he intended to clear the controversy on the royal bloodline saga.

'Could we possibly have descendants of Jesus today?' asked Iscariot.

'Yes, we do.'

'What makes you so sure?'

'Jesus and Mary Magdalene were lovers. She was pregnant with his child at the time Jesus was crucified around AD 33. She was literally crying for a husband at the foot of the cross.'

'Anything in the Bible to support your assertions?'

'The Bible is a biased compilation of books especially the New Testament. It effectively subdues Mary Magdalene trying to show by all means that she was just a follower and not a lover of Jesus. Worse, she was labeled a prostitute simply to make the thought of Jesus making a prostitute pregnant impossible.'

'Anything to support the assertion that the Bible is biased?'

'Yes, the gospels discarded by the early Christian church, basically the Catholic Church, give us a better picture of the intimate relationship between Jesus and Magdalene.'

'Any example?'

'The Gospel according to Phillip.'

'What does it say?'

'It says and I quote, "Jesus used to often kiss her on the mouth".'

'Why was the Gospel of Phillip not made part of the Bible?'

'Because it clearly shows some intimate relationship that existed between Jesus and Magdalene.'

'So what happened to the child Magdalene had in her womb at the cross?'

'Jesus survived the staged killing on the cross and the first person he saw was Mary Magdalene. Mary Magdalene knew Jesus' plans but she feared that if things did not go as planned Jesus could die on the cross.'

'What do you mean by "if things did not go as planned"?'

'The plan was to fake the death of Jesus and then have him escape. Magdalene's fear was the game plan could end up in Jesus actually dying on the cross especially when she saw the scourging of Jesus and the manner in which he was tortured before being hang on the cross.'

'Did her fears come true?'

'Luckily no, the plan worked out and Jesus did not die on the cross.'

'So where did they go after that?'

'Jesus and his followers helped Magdalene escape to Egypt with Joseph of Arimathea in order to protect her and the unborn child.'

'Who is Joseph of Arimathea?'

'He is the one whose tomb Jesus was put in after the staged crucifixion. He too knew the plan and he worked hand in hand with Jesus to assist Mary Magdalene.'

'Did Magdalene then settle in Egypt?'

'No, she went further and ended up settling in the south of France.'

'What happened to Jesus?'

'It is not clear but it seems he preferred to continue his movement in Rome where he finally died around AD 64.'

'Did he have any other children before his death?'

'Some believe he used to link up with Mary Magdalene in France and had more children with her. Others believe the separation made it impossible for the relationship to continue and Jesus could have married another woman in Rome.'

'What happened to the child or children of Jesus?'

'Jesus' first child, a girl, ended up marrying among the Merovingians who later became the French kings.'

'What about his other children?'

'One married in England and the rest married in Rome.'

'This is what made you conclude that Jesus has descendants today in France, Italy and the United Kingdom?'

'Correct.'

'No further questions,' concluded Iscariot.

CHAPTER 41

INAPPROPRIATE RELATIONSHIP

It was not easy to deal with anyone's personal relationships in public. We all want our private lives private. If you were a public figure like Bill Clinton, the Monica Lewinsky story could turn out to be very damaging even if on the surface of it, it simply showed that we were all vulnerable to falling in love. Thumbs up for those that helped Clinton argue his case. Now Magdalene had to deal with an alleged inappropriate relationship between Jesus and Mary Magdalene.

What made things worse was that Magdalene herself was from southern France. Her grand mother used to tell her that she carried royal blood and she thought her grand mother was simply fascinated with the stories of the Merovingians

Kings and wanted to impress her grand daughter. Her surname, Royal, did not help much to dispel her grand mother's assertions. Magdalene ended up settling in United States.

If this story of Jesus' bloodline is true and if Magdalene's grandmother was right, Magdalene is a living example of the bloodline of Jesus. Was this the reason why Jesus chose her to defend him?

Law practice teaches you not to get personally involved in your client's issues. Just stick to the facts and argue out your case. Be professional. Avoid emotions. Stick to the law. But this is the closest Magdalene has come to a conflict of interest. Getting instructions from Jesus on this witness is as good as establishing her identity. What will Jesus say? How is she to avoid being emotional with Jesus? After all, she could be carrying his blood?

What seemed far was now near. She did manage to get instructions from Jesus and the instructions she got were typical of Jesus. The moment of truth has now come. Iscariot had finished his part and it was now time for Magdalene to ask her questions.

'The issue of Jesus' bloodline existed before AD 33?'

'Correct'

'Is there anything in the Bible that gives us a glimpse of Jesus' bloodline?'

'Yes.'

Magdalene handed the witness exhibit 1 and continued asking questions.

'What is that you have in your hands?'

'A Bible.'

'Find the passage that refers to Jesus' bloodline.'

The witness flipped pages to and fro and finally found the passage.

'I have found it.'

'Can you tell us where it is in the Bible before you read it.'

'The first is in the Gospel of Luke Chapter 11 verse 27 to 28.'

'What does it say?'

'I quote, "As he said this, a woman in the crowd raised her voice and said to him, 'Blessed is the womb that bore you, and the breasts that you sucked!' But he said, 'blessed rather are those who hear the word of God and keep it!" end of quote.'

'What does the passage mean?'

'That keeping the word of God is more important than bloodline.'

'Where is the second passage?'

'The second passage is from the Gospel of Luke Chapter 8 verses 19 to 21.'

'Please read the passage for us.'

'I quote, "Then his mother and his brothers came to him, but they could not reach him for the crowd. And he was told, 'your mother and your brothers are standing outside, desiring to see you.' But he said to them, 'my mother and my brothers are those who hear the word of God and do it." End of quote.'

'What does the passage mean?'

'It seems, to Jesus, blood relations are irrelevant. He is more interested in those who do the will of God.'

'Did Mary Magdalene have blood relations with Jesus?'

'Of course not.'

'Did Mary Magdalene have a personal relationship with Jesus?'

'Of course yes.'

'Is there anything wrong with having a personal relationship with Jesus?'

'Not at all.'

'Are there people in France today who have a personal relationship with Jesus?'

'Yes, they are many, more than half the population of France.'

'What about the United kingdom?'

'More than half the population too.'

'And the United States of America?'

'More than two thirds of the population of the USA has a personal relationship with Jesus.'

'Does that mean more than two thirds of the population of USA has any blood relationship with Jesus?'

'No.'

'Why not?'

'It is irrelevant.'

'No further questions.'

Iscariot was stunned. He could not believe what hit him. How could this witness admit that blood relations with Jesus were irrelevant? He could not believe that Magdalene found an escape route. Should he ask in redirect? Is there any chance of this witness mending the damage caused? Iscariot decided to take the risk.

'Do you recall your final answer to a question from defense counsel that blood relations to Jesus were irrelevant.'

'I do recall.'

'Does this mean they are no human beings who exist today who have the blood line of Jesus?' Iscariot asked his disguised question with caution expecting a miracle to happen.

'There could be but that is irrelevant'.

'No further questions,' snapped Iscariot with disappointment.

He cursed himself for taking a chance that simply emphasized the irrelevancy of bloodline. This made Iscariot angry – very angry.

CHAPTER 42

THE FIRST TEST

What a witness and what intelligent cross-examination from Magdalene! I had completely forgotten about the beggar. Iscariot thought he had caught Magdalene napping but she proved tougher than he expected.

It was only when the witness was excused by court that I remembered the appointment with the beggar. I had just enough time to get to my apartment.

I sat in my apartment chair looking at the clock as it ticked away the last seconds before six pm. There was a knock on the door at exactly six. I opened the door and saw a well dressed man clad in a black suit and looking like a typical FBI agent.

'Congratulations Puzio!' he exclaimed, 'You have passed your test'

'What test?' I asked

'The beggar test, better known in Christian circles as the Good Samaritan'

'So that was a test. What if somebody else stopped to help you before I did?'

'You make it sound so easy. Three hundred and sixty eight people passed me by this morning, all lost in their little worlds and only you stopped and helped.'

'Three hundred and sixty eight!'

'Yes, and I bet you a lot of them are Christians. Two thousand years of Christianity and the simple lesson of the Good Samaritan has not been learnt.'

'But there are so many beggars in the streets; you do not expect every Jim and Jack to just stop,' I said partially defending myself because I almost chose not to help.

'Well, this beggar was in pain, beaten up by robbers. He was not asking for a dime but life, someone to save his life.'

'Why did Fr. Perdo give you my name and how did you know my apartment?' I digressed as I added another question before he could answer the first.

'We will get to that later. Your apartment may be bugged; we should go where it is safe.'

Now I was convinced he was some agent investigating the murder of Fr. Perdo. But why would a State agent waste his time giving me a test?

CHAPTER 43

Mysterious House

Before long I found myself being driven in a small sedan vehicle. The fake beggar finally introduced himself as RonaldoVinci.

'Any relationship to Leonardo da Vinci?' I asked.

'Not at all, I always get that question. It seems the only Vinci you people know is Leonardo,' he answered.

He seemed to drive in circles but within thirty minutes he stopped at a place that I was seeing for the first time. He asked me to follow him and I did just that. We entered a thicket of trees and walked in zig-zag to what looked like a simple house on a farm. He pressed some code near the main door before it opened. Inside was a typical home. But he pulled some books from a shelf, pressed other codes and the bookshelf gave way to stairs going down. He asked me to follow him. I was more convinced I was dealing with a State agent. Why such secrecy and codes in a simple house?

The stairs led to what was another house. I saw an elevator showing three floors below. I followed him into the elevator. He placed his hand on a screen in front of him and a voice asked which floor. Vinci answered and we found ourselves three floors down.

The elevator opened to a corridor that led to a conference room. They were twelve seats around a long table. Seats were clearly marked one to twelve and one seemed to be the seat for the leader of whoever met in this conference room.

Something struck me though. There were no names on all the seats except one. Vinci asked me to take a seat on the one with a name. As I moved closer to the seat, I almost lost my breath when I read the name on the seat. Father Perdo.

I could not keep my silence anymore as I sat. This stranger had literally revealed a secret place to me and seemed to trust that I would keep it secret.

'Why have you brought me here?' I asked.

'Good question, now we can talk.'

CHAPTER 44

THE HIDDEN KEY

Vinci first made me a cup of tea as if there was no urgency at all. He ignored the fact that suspense was killing me.

'I have good news for you,' he burst out from nowhere.

'What good news?'

'You, John Puzio, are the chosen one.'

'Chosen for what?' I asked knowing that there was no need to get excited about being chosen for something you did not know.

'You have been chosen to reveal the quest that every Christian seeks,' he said with a big smile on his face.

'What quest?' Do not tell me you are the Priory of Sion and want me to finally reveal the secret about Mary Magdalene.'

'Mary Magdalene is not the key to Christianity.'

'Are you then the Knight Templars?'

'Not at all …'

'Or maybe the survivors of the Knight Templars masquerading under a new name?'

'I like your inquisitive mind. We are neither the Priory of Sion nor the Knight Templars.'

'What are you then?'

'You will soon know but first you must understand the quest that every Christian seeks.'

'What quest?'

'The key to Christianity'

'And what is that key?'

'Jesus'

'But who does not know that the key to Christianity is Jesus. That is nothing new for me to reveal.'

'You are right but there is one key that every Christian seeks.'

'Another key apart from the key to Christianity?'

'Yes, the hidden key'

CHAPTER 45

THE SECRET TO JESUS

I seriously thought there was only one key- Jesus- the only key to Christianity. But here was Vinci talking about another key. He even says it was hidden.

'What is this hidden key that every Christian seeks?' I asked

'The key to Jesus,' answered Vinci.

'The key to Jesus?'

'Yes, the key to Jesus.'

'What do you mean?'

'The key that unlocks Jesus so that every Christian knows him.'

'You mean Jesus is not really known after two thousand years of Christianity?'

'You have hit the nail on the head! There are questions about whether everything about Jesus has been revealed. There are questions too on whether what has been disclosed so far is authentic. Some feel the authenticity of the Bible is questionable because the ones who wrote it and the ones who put it together mixed the truth with their own interests Only the hidden key can reveal the secret to Jesus.'

'Well, I know Jesus is in a prison cell because of all these questions, are you telling me you have the key to get him out?' I asked definitely excited about the key to Jesus.

'The same key to Jesus is the only key that can save him from conviction. As long as the Jurors do not get the key, Jesus will be found guilty.'

'So you want me to give the key to the jurors?'

'To reveal the key.'

'Reveal the key?'

'Yes"

'And then what?'

'Once it is revealed, the jurors will get it.'

'The trial ends in less than ten days. Are you expecting me to reveal this hidden key that I do not know in less than ten days?'

'Yes, I do.'

'How will it be?'

'With God everything is possible. What you have to watch out for is not time but the evil one.'

'What are you saying?'

'The one who killed Father Perdo knew exactly what he was doing. But the person the evil one really wants is not the one he killed but the one chosen to reveal the hidden key.'

'You mean the killer will be after my life.'

'The killer will be after your death.'

CHAPTER 46

DEATH ON MY BACK

The thought of a murderer keen to see that I die sent shivers down my spine. I began to doubt whether it was worth it to trade my life for being the chosen one.

'Do I have a choice whether to accept this quest or not?' I asked Vinci, clearly showing doubt in taking it up.

'This is your test number two Puzio. Keep in mind that even Jesus had a choice whether to accept his quest or not. If you choose not to take it then you are not the chosen one. Take it or leave it.'

I thought quickly about what was happening to Jesus in court. I thought also about the millions of Christians who seek the key to Jesus. I even remembered my parents and wondered how I would have reacted if I met someone with the cure to Aids before my parents died. I would have certainly got the cure and saved my parents. Am I not dealing with a similar issue? Christianity was sick. It was distorted and corrupted and needed a cure. Here before me was the key that would save millions of Christians. Saying no to an offer to reveal the key to Jesus would certainly be irresponsible.

'I will do it,' I replied emphatically to Vinci without even thinking twice about the fact that my life would be in danger. I knew the murderer would be looking for me. I knew that this decision was as good as death on the cross. But this to me would be worth it if I could save millions in their quest to know Jesus.

CHAPTER 47

THE FIRST LESSON

Vinci then spent the next two hours giving me what he called the first lesson of the hidden key. The lesson sounded simple but simple things could sometimes be complex.

'Jesus simply called the lesson 1. The first lesson you should learn Puzio is that YOU ARE GOOD.'

'Well I do not know what you mean by good but I have done a lot of bad things in my life.'

'Puzio, when you were born, you were created good just like Adam and Eve in the garden. Evil was not created in you. It is something you later introduced.'

'You mean the snake introduced to me?' clearly casting my mind to poor Eve in the Garden of Eden.

'No Puzio-.'

'Pardon me, you mean the devil introduced to me,' I quickly corrected myself.

'No Puzio, you introduced to yourself.'

'How?'

'Do not rush. Have you not noticed that there is no baby ever convicted?'

'Come to think of it, you are right.'

'Every baby is good. Every five months, ten months or one year old is good. That is how all of us were created from Asia to Africa, Europe to Australia and the Americas.'

'If we were all born good then where does evil come from?'

'Good question, we create it ourselves and blame it on the devil.'

'Gee, I really want to know how I create evil myself. So everybody, even a terrorist, a murderer and a rapist were born good?'

'Yes Puzio.'

'What went wrong for them to be what they became?'

'That will be your second lesson which Jesus simply called 2. For now say to yourself that you are good. Be happy with yourself and the fact that you were created good. Never mind the evil that came later. Get convinced with good first because it is good that will help you face your own evil. It is good that will help you face the evil one'

CHAPTER 48

THE GOSPEL ACCORDING TO JESUS

'Where are you getting all these lessons?' I asked Vinci suspiciously.

'Jesus gave himself these lessons. There are the ones that made him who he was. And he wrote these lessons.'

'You mean Jesus actually wrote something?'

'Yes, he did.'

'But why then do we not have a Gospel according to Jesus in the Bible?'

'That is the unfortunate thing about the Bible. Somehow the circumstances that led to the putting together of the Bible made them miss the most important part, what Jesus himself wrote.'

'Do these writings exist today?'

'We have them. That is why we are called the defenders of the hidden key. We have preserved these writings for two thousand years now. It is believed that the Vatican has them too.'

'Why has the Vatican not disclosed these writings all these years?'

'Ask them.'

'How did you manage to keep Jesus' writings for so long? Two thousand years is a long time and Christianity has lost a lot of writings through the centuries.'

'You are right but we the defenders of the hidden key have existed for almost two thousand years.'

'Do not tell me! Why then did you not disclose the writings to save the world from all the distortion surrounding the Bible and Jesus?'

'That is the beauty of God. Everything has its own time and the writings were to be released when the world was ready to receive and understand them. The defenders of the key would have all been burnt as heretics but today's world is different. It will not kill you for challenging Christianity.'

'Interesting.'

'Enough for tonight, just keep in mind the first lesson that Jesus taught himself. All human beings are created good whether Gentiles, Samaritans or Jews. Go to court tomorrow and tell yourself that every human being you meet is good. Once you have learnt this come and learn lesson two. Smile at every person. It costs nothing. Just enjoy the fact that you are good and every human being is good whether Tutsi or Hutu, Serb or Croat, American or Arab. All are good.'

CHAPTER 49

THE MASKED MAN

I was dropped back at my apartment late that night. I sat for a while on my bed thinking about the first Jesus lesson I just received. I thought I was born dirty with some kind of curse called original sin. I thought I was evil and then spent my life trying to be good.

But the lesson tells me the opposite. I am good and every human being is good. Name them, the worst you have met and the lesson says they are good. Yes, all those you hate are good. All the murders, genocides, rapes and robberies were committed by people who themselves were good but somewhere on their journey of life lost themselves. No wonder Jesus had no problem associating with the

Samaritans, tax collectors, prostitutes and other outcasts. To Jesus every human being was good. This simply meant to be a follower of Jesus you had to learn to see the good that still existed even in the worst of sinners, in other words, the one you hated most.

I continued sitting on my bed as I tried to let those simple words of lesson one sink in my heart. You are good and every human being is good.

My meditation was abruptly interrupted by a male voice just a meter above my head. I do not know how he entered my apartment and found himself that close to me. The man had a black mask on his face holding a huge razor sharp knife near my throat.

'Do not move unless I tell you so,' he commanded.

'Who are you?' I asked trying to contain my fear.

He simply ignored my question and asked his instead.

'Where is the book?'

'What book?'

'The Mathematics of Jesus.'

'I don't know of a book called The Mathematics of Jesus.'

'The one you call the key to Jesus.'

'You mean that one. I do not know where to find it.'

'You should know, you are the chosen one.'

How did he know so quickly? Did Vinci tell him?

'Who told you I was the chosen one?' I inquired.

'Do not waste my time. I will ask you one more time, where is the book?' he snapped angrily.

'I have not even seen what you are calling the book.'

He looked at me and seemed to believe what I said.

'There is only one copy of the book. Now that you have been chosen to reveal it, you will soon see it. That book will be put in your hands and the only reason I am here is because I want that book.

'I can not give it to you, I do not know where the book is.'

'You do. The place where you went to tonight is the place where the book is.'

'But I do not know how to get to that place.'

'I believe you. Vinci is a clever and shrewd man. He will let you know the place but will not show you how to get there. Even what you saw on the surface has changed by now.'

'What makes you think I would give you the book even if I had it?' I choked a bit as I tried to continue the conversation with a knife on my throat.

'I know you would not. But I also know that you will because what I demand I get. Are you not surprised that I know you, your apartment and what just happened to you tonight? That should be enough to tell you that your life is in my hands. I can kill you right now if I wanted. So go with Vinci when he comes. Go on with his Jesus lessons but remember that as soon as he shows you where the book is I will find you.'

The masked man opened my apartment exit door and simply disappeared into the dark night.

CHAPTER 50

HOLY GRAIL

I had a sleepless night but I managed to wake up in time for trial on day five.

It seemed Iscariot did not want to give up on the "inappropriate" relationship between Jesus and Mary Magdalene. He called another witness to try and regain what he had lost with the witness "NN".

'Your name witness?'

'Dr. Greysham Grey.'

'Your qualifications?'

'I have a masters degree and a doctorate degree.'

What is your specialty in your Masters degree?

'Biblical history.'

'What about your doctorate?'

'The search for Holy Grail.'

'What is Holy Grail?'

'It is a specific woman's womb.'

'Which woman?'

'Mary Magdalene.'

'What did that womb contain?'

'Jesus' child.'

'You mean there was an intimate relationship between Jesus and Mary Magdalene?'

'The womb speaks for itself.'

'No more questions.'

CHAPTER 51

DISBELIEF

Here we go again, thought Magdalene, another attack on Jesus' relationship with Mary Magdalene. She kept her cool and approached the witness with care.

'I have instructions from my client that the Holy Grail refers to his blood, your comment.'

Noise erupted in the stadium court as the crowd looked at Magdalene with disbelief. Did she just say she had instructions that the Holy Grail referred to Jesus' blood? She had effectively agreed to Iscariot's argument on Jesus' bloodline. Magdalene had just admitted what the witness said, or hadn't she?

The stadium court was finally brought to order and the witness was given an opportunity to comment.

'I agree with you, it refers to Jesus' blood,' said the witness.

'When was this link of the Holy Grail to the cup that Jesus used at the last supper made?'

'In the twelfth century.'

'What about the link to Joseph of Arimathea?'

'In the twelfth century too.'

'What was there before the twelfth century?'

'Nothing. There were no Holy Grail stories before that.'

'So where are you getting your Mary Magdalene link?'

'Through the study of Leonardo Da Vinci's works.'

'And when did Leonardo Da Vinci live?'

'From fifteenth to sixteenth century, he was in fact the Grandmaster of the Priory of Sion from 1510 to 1519.'

'You agree with me that the link of the Holy Grail to the womb of Mary Magdalene did not exist a thousand years after Jesus' death?'

'Correct.'

'Could the Holy Grail be something more than a cup?'

'It is more than a cup, as I indicated, it is Jesus' bloodline in Mary Magdalene's womb.'

'Could the Holy grail be Jesus' blood?'

'I answered that already. It is his blood.'

'Jesus' blood?'

'Jesus' blood.'

'Jesus himself?'

'Yes, Jesus himself.'

'So the Holy grail is Jesus himself?'

'Oh – I see. So you thought I meant the Holy Grail was Jesus himself?'

'I am putting it to you as I did before that the Holy Grail is Jesus himself.'

'Umhuum... you could be right. Some say the Holy Grail is something much more...much much more... and that much more could be Jesus himself.'

'No further questions.'

CHAPTER 52

CLEVER AND SHREWD

Vinci came to pick me at six p.m. again. He found me already at my apartment after court had adjourned to Monday the following week.

He drove in circles as usual and I found myself walking in the woods, moving towards the house I had seen last night. To my surprise, the house had changed shape and color. This was exactly what the masked man said would happen. He seemed to know Vinci well.

I was not sure whether I should tell Vinci what happened during the night. I was getting suspicious and confused about sudden turns and twists in what was happening to me.

'You look worried Puzio,' said Vinci as we moved to the conference room.

'Well, I have things to think about.'

'The masked man came to you, did he not?'

Oh my God! I almost pissed in my pants. Vinci knows the masked man was in my apartment. And why did he not come to my rescue? A moment of insanity could have made the masked man slit my throat.

Vinci noticed my surprise but continued asking. 'He wants the book, does he not?'

'Yes he does and you seem to know everything,' I said sarcastically.

'The masked man is a very clever and shrewd man. He will do anything to get the book,' continued Vinci clearly ignoring my sarcasm.'

'That makes two clever and shrewd men with opposing demands on me. But why does he want the book?'

'To destroy it and once he destroys it the key will never be known.'

'Why not make copies of the book instead of risking the destruction of such an important book?'

'Only you, the chosen one, can release the key. We are therefore stuck with the original copy till then. It is a risk we have to take.'

'I feel trapped.'

'You mean decision making is getting tough?'

'Well, yes.'

'Welcome to lesson two.'

'I know what lesson two is.'

'You do, and what is it?'

'Lesson one was on good, so lesson two is obviously on evil,'
I said with certainty.

'Wrong Puzio, you are wrong.'

CHAPTER 53

THE SECOND LESSON

How could I be wrong? It is simply common sense that after any lesson on good the next one should be its opposite- evil. This puzzle made me challenge Vinci immediately.

'If lesson two is not on evil what then is lesson two?'

'Lesson two is on the freedom of choice better known in Christian circles as free will.'

'The freedom of choice?'

'Yes, free will in other words.'

'So what you are saying is lesson two is a choice between good and evil?'

'No Puzio, do not rush. It is a choice to be or not to be.'

'What does that Shakespearean phrase mean?'

'It is a choice to be good or not to be good.'

'Is that not a choice between good and evil?'

'No, God created only good. The Adam and Eve myth says it all. Everything was good. And I suppose you know who created evil?'

'The Devil.'

'No Puzio, I did tell you last night.'

'Oh yes, I remember. It is human beings. I had been indoctrinated so much with the old thinking of the Adam and Eve story; it is kind of hard to change the thinking pattern.'

'Human beings realize they can choose not to be like God and they can live their lives different from what God expects. A life without God is nothing but evil.'

'So an atheist is evil?'

'No, remember the atheist was also created good and can choose to live life with God without knowing it.'

'How?'

'Speed kills Puzio. Take it easy and you will soon know how.'

'But I still want to know why you say it is not a choice between good and evil,' I said still puzzled.

'To understand what I mean you need to understand the difference between truth and lies.'

CHAPTER 54

TRUTH AND LIES

I thought the difference between truth and lies was something that everybody knew. I was sure I knew the difference. But I let Vinci continue with what I thought I knew not knowing that Vinci had a surprise for me.

'Do you know that truth exists on its own but lies depend on truth to exist?'

'No I don't. Explain?' I said truthfully, surprised that I did not pay attention to that fact.

'Tell me a lie,' Vinci teased.

'New York is the capital city of the United Kingdom,' I said.

'What is the capital city of the United Kingdom?'

'London.'

'Do you see that for as long as London remains the capital city of the United Kingdom, the New York statement will always be a lie? To put it differently, to say New York is the capital of the United Kingdom contradicts the truth. So a lie is a parasite. It has no life of its own. It exists only because truth exists and it is a distortion of the truth. Truth is, on the other hand, not a distortion of anything. It is pure, uncorrupted and original. It is simply truth. That is why Jesus could say he was the truth. A lie, on the other hand, is corrupted, distorted and impure. By living against good you distort yourself and become a lie. Do you see now that to tell a lie you first have to have the truth?'

'I do.'

'The same with good and evil, good exists without evil but evil can not exist without good.'

'You mean evil is a distortion and corruption of good.'

'Yes Puzio, I am happy you are getting the point now. Evil is just a parasite of good.

CHAPTER 55

JESUS DECODED GOD

The lessons with Vinci were getting more and more interesting in the midst of the chaos I was experiencing.

'After successfully decoding himself as a human being, Jesus tried to do the impossible,' stated Vinci.

'And what was that he tried to do?' I asked curiously.

'He tried to decode God.'

'Impossible. God can never be decoded.'

'That is what we thought but Jesus took up the challenge.'

'Did he succeed?'

'He did; he G-decoded God.'

'Ahh… So this is where G-decoded comes from. I last heard it from Fr. Perdo. If I am right, G-decoded means God-decoded?'

'You are right but how do you use it with an atheist?' asked Vinci.

'Oh, I see. An atheist does not believe in God, so God-decoded can not work with an atheist.'

'Right again,' agreed Vinci. 'God-decoded cannot work with an atheist but G-decoded can.'

'I thought God-decoded and G-decoded were the same?'

'No. That is why it is called G-decoded and not God-decoded.'

'What then is G-decoded?'

CHAPTER 56

G ⋈ Decoded

'To Jesus G-decoded was the decoding of God because he was a believer. But he noticed that in order to use it when dealing with non-believers you keep the G as G because G as God is meaningless to them.'

'This sounds interesting.'

'To Jesus, there was only one God and that God was G.'

'G as in the first letter of the English word God.'

'Correct. Jesus then saw that the difference between God and Good was zero.'

'Oh yes, I remember that from Fr. Perdo. God has one zero and good has two. So the difference between the two is zero.'

'Correct. So if the difference is zero-'

'It means there is no difference,' I finished the sentence.

'Right, and Jesus had a symbol for this.'

'What was the symbol?'

'G.'

'And what did that stand for?'

'God.'

'Did Jesus have a symbol for good?'

'Yes, it looked exactly like the symbol for God.'

'G?'

'Correct, G.'

'How do you tell the difference between the two symbols?'

'You cannot. There are exactly the same.'

'How does all this connect with what I have learnt before?'

CHAPTER 57

To Be or Not to Be

'Jesus realized he was created G and all he was called to do was live G.'

'What do you mean live G?'

'Jesus had the freedom to either live according to G or abandon it.'

'What did he choose?'

'He chose to live G.'

'Was he successful?'

'To the world's eyes he looked like a failure as he hung on the cross. But to Jesus, he hung on the cross because of refusing to abandon G. Even when he felt abandoned by G he never abandoned G. He hung to G to his death.'

'You mean even when he felt abandoned by God Jesus never abandoned God.'

'Correct, could also mean that he felt abandoned by God but never abandoned good. He stuck to what every human being was called to be, good. And by sticking to good he stuck to God because the difference between God and Good was zero.'

'What happened thereafter?'

'In the end Jesus' life was nothing but a full circle of the life of G.'

'What do you mean by full circle?'

'He never ever did $1 + 2 = 3$. He was the first human being to do it and no one else has managed to live the full circle of G ever since. It is this that made his followers realize after his death that there was no difference between Jesus and God. To know Jesus was to know God and to know God was to know Jesus. Jesus had not only G-decoded himself but G-decoded God. Jesus discovered that God was always a $1 + 2 = 1$ and never $1+2=3$.'

'So what happened on the cross was a test?'

'You could say that. It was his last temptation. Jesus could not abandon G for all the riches in this world, not even for all the power in the world. The last test was to subject Jesus to untold suffering resulting in a shameful death. That too did not make Jesus abandon G.'

'Would I be right to say he actually died for God?'

'You are right. It was a death for God and to die for God was to die for every human being. The reason is simple. Every human being is created G. God is G. To die for G is to die for God and good. Jesus defended both the divine and the human.'

'How does all this connect to the trial?'

CHAPTER 58

JURY G-DECODED

I was curious and really wanted to know how the things I was being taught connected to the trial.

'It is wrong for a Christian to claim ownership of G to the exclusion of all others,' Vinci stressed. 'It is therefore wrong for the Christians in the trial to think they own G to the exclusion of the atheists. Every human being is born G and that G is never taken away. You can decide not to live according to G but that does not destroy the G in you. Remember the difference between truth and lies. Living your life in lies does not destroy the truth.'

'How do you apply all this G-decoded to specific persons in the trial of Jesus?'

'Focus on the decision makers, how many are they?'

'Twelve.'

'Correct, divided into?'

'Six Christians and six atheists.'

'Great. What do the Christians believe in?'

'God'

'And what do the atheists believe in?'

'Good.'

'I am impressed Puzio, you are using your decoding of G well. Now what is the difference between the two?'

'If Christians believe in God and the atheists believe in Good the difference is zero.'

'Correct, and if the difference is zero what does that mean?'

'There is no difference.'

'Great Puzio, you will soon master G.'

'But I am curious Vinci. What exactly is happening with the jurors? Are you telling me they have no differences?'

'In fact there are a lot of differences Puzio – differences deep enough to derail the jurors.'

CHAPTER 59

Mistakes

Any court of law that has jurors that do not have differences should consider itself very lucky. The question was usually not whether there were differences amongst jurors but whether the differences were negligible or not.

'What are the differences amongst the jurors?' I asked.

'Let us take the most stubborn group, the Christians. Mistake number one, they think the atheists are evil,' responded Vinci.

'But why would the Christians think the atheists were evil?'

'Simply because the atheists do not believe in God, but do you see what is wrong with this judgment?'

'No.'

'Absence of belief in God does not mean absence of good, and presence of good means presence of God even in an atheist. God is present in the six atheist's jurors; it is simply that they do not believe that the gift of good is from God. The day they will see that will be the day they will cease to be atheists.'

'Can the Christians change too?'

'Yes they can. The Christians can also lose their faith. In other words, they can stop seeing that God exists and start looking at themselves just as atheists. So belief or non-belief does not make you evil. It is how you relate to G that determines who you are.'

'It is strange that Christians can pass such harsh judgment on the atheists.'

'Well, things are worse than that. More mistakes are being made by the Christians.'

'I am surprised. What mistakes now?'

'The Catholics think they hold the truth. They are looking at their break away Protestant cousins as evil.'

'But why would the Catholics look at Protestants like that?'

'Because they think you can only be a true believer if you were Catholic.'

'Is this happening in the trial as we speak or something that happened in the past?'

'Read the history of Northern Ireland. It is a fight basically between Catholics and Protestants, in other words, a fight between Christian and Christian. Things are much better now but it will take more years to heal the wounds caused by the division. The Catholics on their part started their healing process way back in 1962 at the second Vatican Council but the church is yet to catch up with its Vatican two decisions.'

'But I do not understand. If every human being is born good why treat a fellow Christian like that?'

'The source of the problem is because of the reduction of Jesus to a dogma, doctrine, a church building, a rule or regulation. Once you reduce Jesus to any of these things you end up forgetting the basic Jesus lesson. You are good and every human being is good.'

'What about the other Christian jurors?'

CHAPTER 60

Jurors' Ignorance

Vinci decided to start with the unshakable die-hard juror, Maria Spirit.

'Maria Spirit believes you are not a Christian unless you are born again. Mistake made is to make the phrase "born again" into a rule without looking at its real meaning. To Maria Spirit, the Catholics, Pierre Hugo and Ignatius Brown, belong to an evil church, the Roman Catholic Church, with its leader 666, the beast, better known in Christian circles as the Pope.'

'It is not fair to label a Catholic evil simply because of being Catholic,' I added.

'Correct but it has happened before and does happen even today. Some would argue that the Catholics are just getting what they did to others.'

'What about the juror from Seventh Day Adventist?'

'Sabaday Kingston has his problems too. He is a die-hard believer in the Sabbath. He looks at the Catholics and other Sunday Christian worshippers like Protestants and Baptists as lost pagan worshippers. True worshippers to Sabaday are those that worship on the Sabbath and any one who does not observe the Sabbath is evil.'

'That is not fair either.'

'Not at all, this is another example of not knowing lesson one. You are good and every human being is good. Imagine what difference this would make if the jurors knew the lesson. I hope you see how important it is.'

'I do. What about the Watchtower lady, Whitney Queenston?'

'She is not even considered a Christian.'

'Why?'

'Because she does not believe in Jesus as God'

'But does she believe in Jesus as good?'

'Yes, she does.'

'There is no difference between God and good.'

'Not to some Christians, to believe that Jesus is God is condition number one.'

'But is it not?'

'We have other religions that believe in Jesus as prophet and they do not believe in Jesus as God at all. Jesus did not demand that you believe that he is God. But he did demand that you believe in G. To Jesus, a believer in good is as good as a believer in God as long as both do the will of God.'

'But how do you do the will of God if you are not a believer?'

'Simply live according to G.'

'You mean you can do the will of God without believing in God?'

'Exactly, an atheist can live according to God without believing in the existence of God. Conversion may one day come to that atheist when he realizes that God has been with him all along; that he did all the good things he did because of God. Belief will then come in and reveal that G existed even before he became a believer.'

'Why can we not find something to unite us?'

'That is what Jesus discovered and that is the good news.'

'What happened to the good news?'

'We distorted it. Now is the time to reveal the key so that the good news of Jesus becomes the good news.'

'What good news exactly?'

'That you are good and every body is good.'

CHAPTER 61

Meaning of Good

'Vinci, in the decoding of G, G can be God or Good?'

'Correct.'

'Isn't the meaning of good a problem; good may differ from one community to another?'

'It was a problem before but Jesus gave a clear and unambiguous answer.'

'What then is good?'

'The point is not what good is but what you should do to know that what you are doing is good.'

'I do not understand.'

'Good is to do to others what you would want them to do unto you, in other words, love your neighbor as yourself.'

'Meaning?'

'Meaning human beings know what good is.'

'Do you have an example?'

'Yes, I see someone's cell phone left carelessly on a table and I want to steal it. The G question is "if I left my cell phone carelessly on a table, would I mind someone stealing it?"'

'The answer is obviously yes I mind.'

'So if you do not want someone to steal your phone, do not steal their phone. I repeat, do unto others what you would like them to do unto you.'

CHAPTER 62

VINCI

The ease with which Vinci taught the lessons of Jesus made me curious about him.

'Who are you Vinci?'

'What do you mean Puzio? I thought I gave you my name.'

'How did you end up here in Vinci house? Were you also chosen?'

'Read psalm 151 and you will get your answer,' Vinci answered and left the room.

I went to the bookshelves. There were several Bibles of different versions to select from. I picked one and went straight to the psalms. I flipped the pages in chunks till I saw psalm 150. I then flipped the pages one by one till I found – nothing. There was no psalm 151. How could Vinci fool me? I put back the Bible on the shelf.

Then I saw a strange Bible written "with commentary by Vinci". Out of curiosity, I took the Bible from the shelf and opened it. This time I found it, psalm 151.

It was a mizmor written in alphabetical order. A very interesting one and seemed to talk about a big encounter between Vinci and God.

CHAPTER 63

Psalm 151

The first part of the psalm was a lashing out at God.

And what Kind of a God are you?

Burning people forever and ever

Confusion seems to be your delight

Division gives you great pleasure

Ears you have but don't listen

Fed up with you I make my cry

God my God, away from you I ran

Interesting, Vinci was annoyed with God for delighting in the burning of sinners. But I noticed a twist in the psalm when it reached the next letter H.

However far I ran to you

Indeed you are my only refuge

Jesus your son you sent for us

Kindly gave his life for us

Loving father you can't burn them

Must you condemn those you love?

No God, not you

Only your love speaks for itself

Prodigal father, hear my cry

Quiz me not, I plead with you

Rest my mind

Sinners like me, your son died for

Tease me not

Under whose palms, will I ran to?

Vinci my name only you gave me

Will you surely burn me?

Xylophone music is all I hear

Zealously I will worship you!

What a psalm and what an experience! Vinci really had an encounter with God! As soon as I put the Bible with Vinci's commentary back he walked into the room.

'Did you find the psalm?'

'I did.'

'Now you know who I am and why I am here.'

'Yes, you almost walked out on God.'

'I did walk out on God.'

'But you went back to God.'

'Jesus brought me back to God. That is why I have given my life to him.'

Vinci then showed me something in his hands.

"Here is the Book Puzio. Now it is time for you to have it in your hands. The evil one is waiting. Be careful.'

CHAPTER 64

The Surprise

I could not believe I finally had the book in my hands. I looked at it and looked at it again. I knew that my quest had now begun.

Vinci gave me instructions. My task was to get to the printers and make copies. The masked man could not find me where I was but I knew I was vulnerable as soon as I moved out of Vince house. The masked man might attack me and steal the key. Without the key Jesus would never be known.

Vinci handed me a little note with a specific address for the printers. He dropped me six hundred meters away from the building. His reason was to avoid detection by the masked man but I thought the book was going to be safer if I were dropped at the doorstep of the printing house.

I looked at the note Vinci had given me. *Walk straight on, turn right on the second turn, walk up to a police station sign then turn left. Two hundred meters from the sign is a building on your right hand side with no name. It has a huge Romanesque door with a statute of a key on it. Knock and some one will assist you from there.*

I followed the note as instructed, knocked on the huge Romanesque door and a man with a welcoming smile opened the door. To my surprise, it was someone I got to know quite well lately. Someone I had seen giving an opening addressing in the trial promising that Jesus was going to be found guilty.

'Please come in. I am Iscariot Jones, your host.'

CHAPTER 65

CONFLICT OF INTEREST

'Are you also a member of the defenders of the key?' I asked before even entering the building.'

'Come in and we will talk inside. The evil one may be watching us and we need to print as many copies as possible. We are running out of time,' Iscariot cautioned without answering my question.

I quickly entered the building knowing that the masked man's threat was real. Iscariot took me to a huge room full of printing equipment.

'Is it not a conflict of interest for you to be a prosecutor and at the same time assist in the printing of this book? Is what you are doing allowed under your ethics code?'

'There is no conflict of interest. I am just doing God's work.'

Iscariot switched on the machines and put a lot of ink in the ink compartment.

'I am ready now. Please pass me the book.'

I was about to give him the book when I noticed blood on the upper part of the back of his trousers.

'You are bleeding, did you hurt yourself?'

He welcomed my leading question and gave an emphatic yes.

'If it were not for the printing of this book I would be seeing a doctor now. I fell whilst trying to adjust some of this heavy equipment and hurt myself. I have put a bandage on my thigh and the bleeding has stopped.'

'I envy your dedication to duty,' I finally remarked as I passed on the leather bound book to him. I could tell he was seeing it for the first time. He kissed it twice and his angelic smile suddenly turned devilish as he spoke in a voice I had heard before.

'I told you Puzio, that I would find you when you had the book.'

CHAPTER 66

THE MURDERER

I still could not believe my eyes as I stood like a statue.

'Oh my God, oh Jesus Christ!' I looked with shock. 'You, Iscariot, are the masked man…you murdered Fr. Perdo … you shit…'

'Yes Puzio, now you know. You are the only one alive who knows this. Not even Vinci knows this,' replied Iscariot without showing any offence to the last word I had uttered.

'Please can I have the book back?' I demanded, still angry with him.

'Puzio, did you not hear what I said? You are the only one alive who knows who the masked man is. The rest are dead,' he said with a cold heart.

'I heard you clearly. I simply want the book back.'

'You Christians are slow to learn. Worry about your life and not this book. You are a dead man Puzio.'

'Well, I am still alive as you can see,' I retorted stubbornly.

'Not for long courageous little fellow, not for long'

'What makes you think I will just stand here and let you kill me?'

'No, you would not. I love cat and mouse chase. At the end of it I always kill the mice.'

I could have tried to run away. But it would be useless to run without the book. If only I could find a way to get back the book I would give him a hell of a mouse chase.

From nowhere I heard a loud groaning sound as a man pushed open the door to the printing room. He fell to the ground bleeding heavily. I could see stigmata signs showing clearly that someone had rammed nails into his hands and feet. I tried to rush to assist the man but Iscariot pulled a .48-millimeter pistol and ordered me to stay away.

'So you have risen from the dead,' Iscariot teased him.

'Puzio, whatever this man does, do not leave without the book,' said the man in his last breath.

Iscariot shot the man twice in between his eyes and another two shots in his heart in quick succession without remorse.

'I hope I do not have to do this to you Puzio,' he said as he moved closer to me, pointing the gun straight at my face.

CHAPTER 67

HELD HOSTAGE

Iscariot then took my cell phone to make sure I did not communicate with anybody. He also took my wallet so that I did not have money to book a cab in case I escaped. I thought of hitting him but this was wishful thinking with Iscariot holding a pistol next to my head. The precision with which I saw him shoot the unknown man barely minutes ago simply meant he would not miss this close.

'What use is this book to you?' I asked pretending to be a hostage negotiator trying to save the life of a book.

'I can shoot you now and you would die. No one, not your girlfriend, your aunties nor uncles will see you again because you have never died before. But shooting Jesus is useless. He died already but he is sitting in that stadium courtroom still alive and making a mockery of all the evil that exists. The best way to eliminate Jesus is to annihilate the thought of his existence. If all Christians today were convinced that Jesus was dead, he would be dead. It is no longer a fight of flesh and blood. It is a fight against life after death and that book stands in my way.'

'How does eliminating the book assist you?'

'This book is the key young man. I thought Vinci explained all this to you. For as long as Christianity goes away from Jesus it is dead. But this key reveals the secret to Jesus. Once Christians know the secret to Jesus I would have two billion, hardheaded Christians viciously following Jesus. I like lukewarm and blind Christians lost in their doctrines, dogmas and rituals busy squabbling about who is right and who is wrong. The key to Jesus will make Christians stronger and that is the last thing I want.'

I did not know how long this conversation with a man holding a gun on my head was going to last but so far so good. Just keep him talking till a way out was found .

'I see your point,' I concurred.

'Look at what happens when you put six Christians together. Head butts, kicks, insults, this is a mockery to Jesus and I like it. I will encourage it till those Christian jurors fall. When they fall I win and Jesus loses.'

'You seem to like challenges,' I interjected as I noticed the pride with which he loved a good fight.

'I do and I take them head on. Jesus is the biggest challenge I have ever faced.'

'So you have what you want. You are busy persecuting Jesus.'

The tone of his voice suddenly changed and I felt the pistol inch closer as he asked angrily.

'Did you say persecuting Jesus?'

'Pardon me that was a slip of the tongue. What I meant to say was you are prosecuting Jesus, so you have what you want.'

'No I do not have. Prosecuting him without winning is useless. I have to win this case. That would be my most precious prize. Jesus has to be found guilty,' he mumbled on.

'But why is your mind pre-determined? Have you not considered that he could be innocent?'

'You will be charged with contempt young man. You are now discussing the outcome of the case.'

'I am sorry. Here is a challenge for you,' I thought quickly. 'Let me go and see if you can catch me,' I said risking two clean bullets in my head.

'I accept your challenge Puzio. In fact I will make it more interesting. Here is your book and I will find you just the same way I found you. This time there would be no second chance.'

I looked at him dumb founded. I did not expect this and he certainly caught me with my pants down. What do I do next?

CHAPTER 68

Saved from Death

I walked to the main door still expecting gunshots. I opened it and run for my life. Iscariot did not even bother to look. He seemed so sure of himself.

How foolish, I thought to myself. A clever prosecutor with more than thirty years experience in convicting criminals had made his biggest mistake. He had set an eyewitness to his cold blooded murder free. How foolish.

With no money and no cell phone, I had to try and find the nearest police station. I saw three young men nearby with cell phones in their hands. This could be my lucky chance. I quickly went to them asking for direction to the nearest police station. They looked at me, screamed in unison and ran for their lives. I could not understand why. I finally found myself at a police station after a thirty-minute trial and error search. My panic had made me forget that Vinci's directions had included a police station sign.

As I entered the building I relaxed and thought of what the news would be the next day. Chief prosecutor arrested for the murder of two people.

The police officer at the reception area came quickly to attend to me. He looked at me and thought he had seen a ghost. He subdued his reaction and asked me to wait for just a minute.

He went to another room to make a phone call. It was then that my eyes came face to face with a picture of my face pinned on the notice board. The notice clearly stated that I was wanted for the murder of Fr. Perdo and another man they named Tony Brown. Is this why people were running away from me? Then I remembered my wallet and cell phone. Shit, Iscariot could have planted them at the crime scene. I should have expected that. He is not so foolish after all.

By the time the police officer came to attend to me I was a hundred and forty meters away from the police station. I ran like a mad man not knowing where I was going. I had only one question in mind. Where the hell was Vinci?

CHAPTER 69

REJECTION

My panic made me think of a lawyer. I ran to Magdalene's house and rang the bell. Magdalene opened the wooden door but kept her grill door locked. Before I could say anything, she looked at me and quickly banged the door and locked it.

I knew she had recognized me just like those three young men who ran away. I stood still feeling dejected and alone. I turned away from the door and started walking aimlessly. I heard a door suddenly open and Magdalene stood at the doorway with a pistol pointed at me.

'John Puzio, what do you want at my house, the police are looking for you?' she asked still pointing the gun at me.

'Pardon me Madam, please believe me, I did not kill Fr. Perdo and Tony Brown.'

'Then let me call the police to come and pick you here.'

'No madam, the police will not believe my story.'

'And who do you expect to believe your story, me?' she asked suspiciously.

'Please madam, at least give me a minute to explain.'

'Try me, you have your minute,' she said generously.

'Iscariot Jones is the one who killed both Fr. Perdo and Tony Brown.'

'Which Iscariot Jones?'

'The Chief prosecutor in the trial of Jesus'

'Now you are joking,' she giggled. 'Even though he is my opponent in the Jesus trial Iscariot is a professional man who sticks to his ethics. He is a respected lawyer and I have no reason to believe otherwise.'

'Believe me, I am telling the truth.'

'The problem with the truth is that you cannot see it when it comes out of a mouth. Your truth might as well be a lie. Just turn yourself in.'

'Iscariot has corrupted the police's mind. They will not believe my story.'

'Your minute is over. I don't believe you either and good night,' she said as she banged her door and a dead silence followed.

I could hear her talking to the police on her phone. She was shouting deliberately so that I could hear if I was still at her door. She told the police exactly what had happened and said she feared for her life. She even demanded for security to be sent immediately.

I remembered innocent Jesus alone on the cross and how he cried out "my God, my God, why have you forsaken me?" I felt forsaken too; Magdalene does not believe me; and Vinci–yes- Vinci was nowhere to be seen.

CHAPTER 70

LESSON THREE: EVIL

I walked to my apartment still feeling dejected. I quickly turned back when I saw two police officers hanging around the building. I looked at the parking lot and saw two strange vehicles parked. It seemed my apartment was under surveillance.

Suddenly I heard a noise and somebody shouted, "There he is!". I turned to see who said this and saw an officer with two others running towards me.

I ran for my life.

There was a crazy chase. One officer ran faster than the rest. He caught up with me and grabbed the back of my jacket. Then I realized I was near familiar woods. Vinci woods. That inspired me to let go of my jacket, made a quick right turn and disappeared into the woods.

I continued running, not knowing whether the officers were still chasing me. I felt my legs giving up and decided to hide in a nearby thicket. I was so tired that I subsequently dozed off in the cold. If what was happening to me was a nightmare, my dream was worse. I was awoken by five police officers with guns pointed at me. I screamed and realized it was just a nightmare when I finally awoke only to find Vinci telling me to wake up. I was so happy to see him; I forgot to show my anger for his absence.

He told me to follow him and I did. Before long we passed what seemed to be the thick forest I was now getting familiar with. It did not take long for us to reach the house –yes- looking different again.

Vinci made sure I was warm and gave me something to eat; I had not eaten the whole day. After he noticed that I was relaxed, he looked at me the way he always did when he was about to ask a question.

'I suppose you have something to tell me.'

'Oh… so you did not know this time?' I snapped.

'He threatened you with a razor sharp knife and a gun?'

I did not know whether to get annoyed or just ignore what Vinci had just said. How did he know all this?

'Yes, he did threaten me with a knife and killed Tony Brown. Nothing good has happened. It is all evil.'

'Welcome to lesson three –Evil.'

CHAPTER 71

The Devil

'Are these things I have experienced this evening part of my lessons?' I asked Vinci suspecting that he could be setting me up with Iscariot just to teach me a few lessons.

'No Puzio, it is life itself. Every human being is faced with choices; other human beings you encounter may choose not to live according to G. The evil that results from their choices affects the innocent followers of G. Jesus did not do anything wrong but the wrongdoers' actions resulted in him being hung on the cross. This is the challenge we face every day. We have a mission to change the hearts of those that turn away from G. We have a mission to save them.'

'What is the connection between evil and the famous name that contains the word evil in its spelling – Devil?'

'Let us start from the beginning. I think you know by now that everything good is from God and not a single evil thing comes from God?'

'That I know, you taught me in lessons one and two.'

'But what you have learnt in lessons one and two is not how God was understood in the early history of the Israelites.'

'You mean they had a different understanding of good and evil?'

'Correct. Their first understanding which you see in the Old Testament was that there was only God and the Devil did not exist at all.'

'I do not understand you. The Devil is in the Bible right at the beginning, in the book of Genesis. I can quote you the verses if you want.'

'But the book of Genesis is not the first book –.'

'But it is and we all know that,' I exclaimed, clearly surprised by Vinci's ignorance.

'Be patient Puzio, I have not finished. Even though Genesis is the first book in the order of the books in the Bible, it was one of the last Old Testament books to be written.'

'You mean, if we had to put the books in the Bible in the order in which they were written Genesis would be one of the books just before the New Testament?'

'Correct. That is why Genesis sounds like a New Testament book when it comes to understanding evil. Genesis has a Devil or Satan and the Devil is all over the New Testament.'

'If it is Genesis that introduced the Devil in the New Testament, what existed before?'

CHAPTER 72

EVIL WITHOUT THE DEVIL

We are all curious about how life was without the Devil. If the Devil did not exist but evil did, where was this evil coming from? It is this puzzle that had made me ask Vinci.

'Good question, God was seen as the one having both good and evil,' explained Vinci.

'No… how can they associate God with evil?' I asked with shock

'It was not that they thought God was evil –no- they simply thought good and evil were things God had in possession.'

209

'But what use was evil to God?'

'The Israelites believed that those who turned their backs to God were punished by evil from God.'

'But how did God then decide who to punish with evil?'

'The one who had sinned was the one they believed God punished; the bigger your sin the bigger your punishment. If misfortune came your way, whether through death of a close member of your family or loss of any of your possessions like sheep, society judged you as a sinner. Even natural disasters like the Tsunami would have been considered a curse from God for sin.'

'How different is this understanding from G-decoded?'

'In G-decoded God is good and has nothing to do with evil. In the old understanding, God has both good and evil and uses evil power to punish sinners. In G-decoded, evil is a distortion of good and has no power in itself. In the old understanding evil is as powerful as good and both belong to God.'

'But how did the Devil come in?'

'Do not rush. I hope you understand how people confused God with evil.'

'I do.'

'That is why we ended up with an image of some tyrant God with a big whip who could not wait to punish a sinner. But questions arose in the Old Testament on whether the evil punishment came from God.'

'Any example?'

'The book of Job is a classic on this. The writer depicts Job as a human being who never sinned and yet faced with the worst disasters that could ever happen to anyone. He lost his children and all his wealth. As if this was not enough, God even cursed him with sickness.'

'Did Job complain?'

'He complained bitterly. His friends were convinced Job had sinned against God for God to give him such evil and persuaded Job to just repent to God. But Job refused because he was convinced he had no sin and instead challenged his friends and God to explain why he, as innocent as he was, had to suffer so much. You can clearly see that the writer was challenging the understanding of his society that God moved around with evil and sent it to punish sinners.'

'What happened in the end?'

'The writer himself had no answer to the question. Instead, he contradicts himself at the end and makes God give back to Job all that God had taken away as if to say that God did cause evil except that a mistake was made by God on Job!'

'So the story of Job ends just like that?'

'Yes, that is why people could not understand why Jesus, the innocent one, was punished by God on the cross. They tried, just like in Job's story, to figure out what sin caused God to punish Jesus so severely with evil.'

'That sounds distorted.'

'Of course yes. The understanding of evil was distorted and the distortion got worse.'

'Got worse?'

'Yes, got worse.'

'How?'

CHAPTER 73

DISTORTION OF EVIL

Vinci paused a bit before responding. It is bad enough to have one distorted understanding of evil. It would certainly get worse if the distortion was compounded by another distortion. I looked at Vinci expecting an answer to how the distortion of evil got worse.

'A new answer was found to explain who caused evil,' he finally said.

'I am curious. What was the new answer they found?'

'That evil was caused by the Devil.'

'Who is the Devil?'

'The Bible introduces the Devil as an angel who was banished from heaven. So things had changed from God causing both good and evil to God causing only good and the new face- the Devil- causing evil.'

'Was this a distortion also?'

'Yes it was. Human beings, like in the story of Adam and Eve, were seen as being pulled by two forces; good from God and evil from the Devil.'

'What is the problem of this understanding?'

'It makes human beings not take responsibility of their sin.'

'I see... any example?'

'Look at Adam and Eve. Adam blamed Eve and Eve blamed the Devil. In the end Adam and Eve were actually telling God that if God had not created the Devil they would never have sinned.'

'Is that excuse not correct?'

'No Puzio, remember G-decoded. As long as we have the freedom not to choose G, sin can happen. So it is not the Devil who is the problem, it is our freedom of choice. It is a matter of to be or not to be G.'

'What would happen if God took away our freedom of choice?'

'Then they would be no more sin but we would also cease to be human. Freedom of choice is what makes us human.'

'How does all this connect with Jesus?'

'Jesus' society had a mixture of the two distorted understandings of good and evil. Many passages in the gospels show how Jesus had difficulty explaining to the people that misfortune was not a punishment from God.'

'Any example?'

'Yes, the story of the man born blind. '

'He also had a problem explaining to the people that sin came from them. Of course he was using G-decoded.'

'So it is not the Devil that is making Iscariot kill?'

'Not at all, Iscariot has murdered because he chose to murder. He exercised his freedom not to listen to G. He is fully responsible for his decisions. Fr. Perdo did not die because God took his life as a punishment for sin. It is simply because another human being, Iscariot, chose to abandon G and kill. The same with the murder of Tony Brown; the innocent die not because of their sin but because of someone's choice not to follow G. God has given us a lot of power. It is not only power to decide about ourselves but the freedom to do with the earth what we like. That is why countries are now sensitive to climate change, ozone layer and the preservation of endangered species. It is all because if we, human beings, do not preserve our planet we should not blame it on God. It is the turning of our backs on G that makes us destroy the earth.

'Puzio, time has come for you to stop running and hand yourself to the police.'

'But you know I did not murder Fr. Perdo and Tony Brown.'

'Jesus was innocent too but did not run away from the law.'

'I will report myself first thing in the morning. I am ready to face the police.'

'Very wise Puzio. But now is the time for you to do the final test.'

'Oh no Vinci. Not another test.'

CHAPTER 74

THE MATHEMATICS OF JESUS

'What is 1+2 Puzio?'

'Do not make me laugh Vinci. That is simple kindergarten maths.'

'You have finished the three Jesus lessons. But the lessons are incomplete if you do not answer the simple kindergarten mathematical question. What is 1+2?

'Are you serious?'

'Your life depends on it.'

'But everybody knows the answer to that simple question.'

'Puzio, what is 1+2?'

'3.'

'Wrong, try again.'

'It can only be 3.'

'Wrong Puzio, think.'

'I can not think beyond what everybody knows. 1+2 is equal to 3.'

'Your mind is blocked. You have stopped thinking.'

Suddenly an alarm went off. Windows and doors started shutting automatically. But one glass door was smashed and the masked man stood in front of us with a pistol in each hand pointed at Vinci and me.
'It is Iscariot Jones,' I screamed.'He is hiding behind the black mask.'

'Don't panic Puzio. This is a distraction. He wants you to panic. Concentrate on the question. What is 1+2?'

'You can't answer it young man. The Jesus lessons have blocked your mind. You are a failure. You are just some sinner who is no use to God. I told you I would find you again. Hand over the book.'

'Leave me alone Iscariot. I know it is you. Shoot me if you want.'

'Relax Puzio. You are doing exactly what he wants. You need to control your anger to beat him. This is not a fight of the flesh. It is a battle of the mind. Ignore the pistol. Think.'

'I can't think Vinci. I can't think anymore.'

'Open the book,' commanded Vinci.

'But…'

'Don't worry about him. He also wants you to open the book.'

I looked at Iscariot with fear. He stood still and silent as if agreeing with Vinci. I quickly removed the leather cover and opened the book. Inside the book was a key.

'Check under the key and you will see a key hole,' instructed Vinci.

He was right. It was clear the key was meant to open a small door.

'Open the small door Puzio. Do it now.'

I took the key with fear and it dropped. I looked at the masked man and he still stood silent. I quickly picked the key and opened the small door. Inside was a warning. It read "Do not open this page if you are not the chosen one".

'You know what you are. Do what you must,' said Vinci.

'I flipped the page and it read "You have only one minute in which to answer the question on the following page. Only the correct answer will reveal the hidden key"'

'Do not flip the page if you are still angry. Rid your thoughts of all evil,' warned Vinci.

I did not care anymore. I just flipped the page and there before my eyes was a stop watch with 60 on it.I blinked and the number had changed to 59 within a second. I realized the count down had began. I quickly looked for the question and found it.

What is 1+2?

'Oh my God. The same question that Vinci was asking me. If 3 was wrong then I am in trouble. Big trouble.'

There was a sudden squeaky laugh from the masked man.

'The countdown has began and you will never find the answer to the question. You are a loser,' tauted the masked man.'

'Don't confuse me Iscariot.'

'Think Puzio. Think of the 3 lessons,' advised Vinci.

'Rubbish,' said Iscariot, 'total rubbish.'

'I am trying Vinci but I can't think anymore. Please help me.'

'Just say 3 young man. Just say 3,' laughed the masked man. 'You have only 20 seconds left and I will leave you in your misery. He smashed a window and disappeared into the dark night still shouting 3-3-3.

'Ignore his distraction. Concentrate on the lessons of Jesus. What is 1?' asked Vinci

'1 is good.'

'What is 2?'

'2 is the power to choose 1 or not.'

'So if 2 chooses 1 where will you be.'

'At 1.'

'Then what is 2+1?'

'Oh my God, O my God! 2+1=1. So 1+2=1!'

'Correct Puzio. Welcome to the mathematics of Jesus! You have done it!'

CHAPTER 75

DAY SIX

Day six of the trial was a quiet Monday morning. Knowing that Magdalene literally conceded to Jesus confessing to be the Son of God, Iscariot called another witness to try and show that Jesus' claim to be the Son of God was false. He was not bothered about the hidden key because he was sure Puzio had failed the test.

'Your name witness.'

'Dr. Vaticano Giliano.'

'Your qualifications?'

'I have a Masters in theology and a doctorate in church history.'

'Have you ever heard of the Council of Nicaea?'

'Yes, I have. I did my doctoral dissertation on it.'

'What was it?'

'It was the time that Jesus was made into God.'

'Can you elaborate?'

'Jesus was not looked at as a Son of God or God before the Council of Nicaea. In short, he was not seen as divine. It was therefore decided that Jesus be elevated to God.'

'Who decided that?'

'The Catholic Church.'

'Who gave them the mandate to do that?'

'Themselves.'

'No further questions.'

CHAPTER 76

JESUS: ℿERE ℿORTAL

Magdalene stood up. The issue of Jesus being elevated from mere mortal to divine was tricky. A clear separation had to be done between fact and confirmation of an existing fact. She faced the witness and started asking in direct.

'Do you know the seven natural wonders of the world?'

'Yes, I do.'

'Then you know the Victoria falls.'

'Yes I do.'

'Who discovered the Victoria falls?'

'David Livingstone.'

'When?'

' 1835. '

'Where are you getting all this information?'

'From history books.'

'Was David Livingstone the first person to see the Victoria Falls?'

'No.'

'They were people living near the Victoria Falls who saw it before he did.'

'Correct.'

'In fact, they had a name for the Victoria Falls called Musi O Tunya?'

'Correct.'

'Musi O Tunya means the smoke that thunders.'

'Correct.'

'So David Livingstone discovered what was already discovered?'

'Correct.'

'Dr David Livingstone's announcement to Europe that he had discovered the Victoria Falls was simply a putting on paper something that existed before?'

'Correct.'

'David Livingstone's meeting did not create the Victoria Falls but just acknowledged its existence.'

'Correct.'

'If Jesus was divine and some people sat and put that in writing, would that be creating Jesus into a God?'

'Not at all, you can not create what is there already.'

'So you support the theory that Jesus was created into a God because to you Jesus is not divine at all.'

'Correct.'

'Would your conclusion change if you believed Jesus was divine?

'Then I would conclude that what the Council of Nicaea did is simply express on paper what already existed.'

'No further questions.'

CHAPTER 77

The Trinity

Here we go again, thought Iscariot. Another argument by Magdalene based on the supposition if. This was such an empty argument. The fact that it was based on a supposition made it weak unless Magdalene was going to surprise everyone and make her supposition fact.

But how was Magdalene going to prove that Jesus was God? Nobody had been able to do this for almost two thousand years. The Trinitarian explanation of three persons in one God had not made the explanation any easier. It was so complicated that in the end, the ones that use it simply say it was mystery and use mystery to justify why we do not understand their explanation.

Well, this was a trial and no court of law was going to accept any mystery garbage explanation. It wants facts. Was there any human being out there who had a much simpler explanation? Was there any living soul that could give us an explanation that could make us understand the mystery in simple day-to-day language? Short of such magic meant Magdalene was heading for defeat. She better dig deeper, very deep, to find the world's simplest explanation to the world's most complex question, is Jesus God?

CHAPTER 78

Freemasons and G

The next witness was one Iscariot could not wait to testify. This witness held the key to the destruction of Magdalene's defense – G.

Iscariot had been searching the World Wide Web day and night in order to find something he could use to discredit G way before trial began. He had heard about G but did not know exactly what it meant. What he knew was that Magdalene would try to use G as her main weapon in the trial. Iscariot therefore had to find something that would give G a repulsive meaning and pre-empt the meaning that Magdalene might attach to it. It did not take long for him to get a hit. Iscariot remembered his big smile when he had read what he saw as his latest weapon in his war with Magdalene. Freemasons. After all, the Freemasons played an important role in the war that led to the liberation of the United States of America. He too could use them to fight.

The Freemasons are a secret organization with over four million members worldwide. They claim to be non-aligned to any religion. Any male can join them as long as he is a believer whether Christian, Muslim, Hindu or Buddhist.

The method of joining them is secretive and how one moves through the different stages to be finally accepted as a member is also secretive.

Hidden deep in their secret houses are symbols and amongst them is the letter G. This was Iscariot's main interest and he knew exactly how he was going to use it to destroy the last rope Jesus' lawyer was holding to.

CHAPTER 79

THE DEATH RITUAL

D r. Freeman Fraser walked into the stadium court and was introduced as an expert on symbolism.

'Does the capital G letter have any symbolism?'

'Yes it does.'

'Which organization uses the symbol G?'

'The Freemasons.'

'Who are the Freemasons?'

'They are a secret society.'

'What do you mean by secret?'

'Their rituals are kept secret.'

'How big is this secret society?'

'They have about five million members world wide.'

'When did this secret society start?'

'It has been in existence for centuries. As far back as 1717, four Masonic lodges came together in London's banking industry and formed the grand lodge.'

'What is a lodge?'

'It is a building where freemasons carry out their rituals; the equivalent of a church to Roman Catholics.'

'Explain the example about the Catholics?'

'The Roman Catholics are identified by their massive churches which they use for their rituals. The difference between them and the freemasons is that the Catholics ritual is open to the public but not the Masonic ritual.'

'So what happened to the grand lodge you mentioned earlier?'

'It is at this time that a constitution, regulations and symbols were implemented for freemasons.'

'Is this the only grand lodge they have?'

'No, there is another one in New York.'

'Do you have any personal experience of this secret organization?'

'Yes, I used to be a member.'

'For how long?'

'Less than a year.'

'When did you leave?'

'Just a few months ago.'

Why did you leave?

'I was in a Masonic lodge when I heard the secret words of the Master Mason.'

'What was this secret word?'

'Hah nah birth.'

'What does this mean?'

'I hold the instruments of death.'

'So the Master Mason was announcing that he held the instruments of death.'

'Yes.'

'Where you attending a death ritual?'

'It seemed so. Two men were moving behind the initiate. The Master Mason was busy hitting the initiate on the head with a hammer shouting die- die. Then I saw the initiate die.'

'What do you mean you saw him die?'

'I did not see any blood but those two huge men with a tent like blanket wrapped the dead man in it and carried him away.'

'What happened next?'

'I ran away and vowed not to be a member of a murderous organization.'

'From your experience, what do freemasons do?'

'What else but sacrificing human beings in Masonic murder rituals? That is what I saw with my naked eyes.'

'Any documented evidence of human beings sacrificed by freemasons?'

'Their rituals are so secretive that all the evidence is hidden.'

'Did you have a chance to see their symbols?'

'I did, among the many symbols were some funny aprons and a capital G.'

'Did you say a capital letter G?'

'Yes, that was their most important symbol.'

'So you saw the symbol G being used to sacrifice human beings in Masonic lodges?'

'Correct.'

'G similar to the G being used by the defense team?'

'Correct.'

'No further questions.'

CHAPTER 80

EVIL EXPOSED

Not a sound in the stadium court. G had been attacked. Magdalene knew what Iscariot's aim was.

Shaka Chaka was the first victim of Iscariot's G manipulation. He remembered one peculiar incident that happened four years ago in his home village. The village was awoken before dawn by the sound of alarm drums. Members of the village knew that something was wrong. The beat of the drums was one of death, human sacrifice or witchcraft. It was rarely heard but when such sounds were heard everyone was caught in fear as they rushed to the place where the sound of the drums was coming from to witness with their own eyes the tragedy.

That time the tragedy was a woman of middle age whom the chief alleged was caught in the act of witchcraft. She was paraded naked to show that no normal adult human being would walk around naked in the village.

The village witchdoctor was brought to the scene with his charms and two helpers. The helpers gave the witchdoctor two chickens, one black and the other one white. The witchdoctor decapitated the heads of the two chickens in full view of his audience and sprinkled the blood shooting in spasms from the chicken necks on to the woman as the helpers sang war cries and beat their drums.

In the end, the witchdoctor declared and confirmed the woman as a witch of a clan of vicious witches called the Madogos. Her intention was to kill the first-born son of the chief. By this time the news had spread to neighboring villages and the crowd had increased tremendously.

There was a cry from the crowd that the witch be given the punishment of the witches. The chief signaled that they go ahead. The witchdoctor and his helpers took one long wooden stick and pushed it through the woman's anus deep into her body till it pierced her heart. She died instantly. The village cheered and sang songs of victory with the chief, the witchdoctor and his helpers at the forefront.

Two hours later, the police appeared at the scene. After an hour of questioning the people on the cause of the death of the woman, the chief, the witchdoctor and his two helpers were taken to the police station for further questioning. They admitted having killed the woman and their only defense was that she was a witch.

The four ended up charged with the murder of the woman. The High court found them guilty of the murder ten months later and they were sentenced to life. Shaka Chaka's village was stunned. They feared the Madogos even more for they could not understand how the power of the dead witch managed to twist the ignorance of the police and the High court to convict what they thought were innocent men. Little did they know that the "innocent men" used the witchcraft story to hide the truth.

CHAPTER 80

Truth Revealed

The true story was that the witchdoctor and his two helpers sneaked into the village a concubine to satisfy the chief's numerous adulterous affairs. This was at the request of the chief. The chief's plan had not worked this time.

His wife had heard funny groaning sounds in a hut reserved for visitors. She had tried to wake up her husband, the chief, only to find him missing. She did not know that he was busy enjoying the fruits of his adulterous plan.

She had gone nearer to the visitors' hut, which was supposed to be empty, and confirmed that the groaning sounds were of a male and female. The chief's wife started shouting on top of her voice for help. The chief recognized his wife's voice and realized his cover was blown. He knew he had to act fast. He quickly put on his clothes, took the lover's clothes and threw them outside through a window to the surprise of the woman who also wanted to quickly dress up. The chief then immediately joined his wife's scream except his scream was different. It was a cry that you use when you had caught a witch.

The witchdoctor and his helpers knew that things had gone wrong. One of the helpers rushed to pick the woman's clothes that the chief had thrown outside and hid them. The two helpers then joined the chief making the same cry as him. The three male cries drowned the chief's wife's cry for help. This was how the scene changed from a husband caught in the act of adultery to a woman caught in the act of witchcraft.

The chief summoned the witchdoctor who quickly turned up to help cover up the chief's mischief that he was a part of. This was how the innocent woman was murdered.

You may think this was barbaric but ask yourself what the Catholic Church did to Galileo? To Shaka Chaka, Christianity was as guilty as his village witchcraft tricks. This was but one example of how witchcraft was manipulated by those who caused evil to hide their guilt and sacrifice innocent ones in their place.

Evil was simply a lie, a big lie. The chief lied. The witchdoctor lied. His helpers lied. The innocent one died.

Shaka Chaka could sympathize with the death of Galileo. An innocent soul murdered to cover up the truth and perpetuate a lie. Shaka Chaka remembered the saying " a lie is like a short blanket; you cover the head and your feet pop out; you try and cover the feet and your head pops out". How true, thought Shaka Chaka, a lie was not big enough to cover the truth. It could cover parts of the truth but the feet or head will always pop out and it is that that would make the people one day to uncover the blanket and see the truth like what happened to the witchcraft story in Chaka's village and the Galileo story.

The witchcraft incident happened ten years ago. A lot of things had changed since then. Electricity had reached the villages and this had effectively reduced witchcraft. Chaka soon realized that it was witchcraft that had been reduced but not evil. Evil had increased but in a different form. Now the police investigated; someone was arrested and forensic experts examined a body. People who used to be witches before were now sitting behind bars serving sentences for murder.

Chaka remembers too visiting the Livingstone museum in Zambia just a few kilometers from the famous Victoria Falls. On display in the museum was a small wooden gun with beads around it said to be the weapon of a witch. The people alleged to have been killed by such guns had no gun shoot wounds. Chaka suspected their victims were not shoot but poisoned. With the availability of actual guns, Witches were now shooting their victims with AK47 rifles and bullets wounds could now be seen.

What had changed? Nothing. The witch's deception was over and his evil was now exposed. Yes, exposed just like the Freemasons. Freemasons were witches, concluded Shaka Chaka before he could hear Magdalene's cross-examination.

CHAPTER 82

IN DEFENSE OF G

Magdalene stood up in defense of G. She knew that some of the jurors were caught in Iscariot's G manipulation.

'Do you know God-decoded?' asked Magdalene.

'Not at all, it is the first time I am hearing it,' answered Freeman.

'Do you know Good-decoded?'

'No.'

'Do you know G-decoded?'

'I know G but not G-decoded.'

'Does your G stand for good?'

'No.'

'Does your G stand for evil?'

'No- it is obvious that G is not the first letter of the word evil.'

'So your G is the first letter of something?'

'Correct.'

'Does it stand for the first letter of G in the word God?'

'No.'

'What then does it stand for?'

'Geometer.'

'Is this Geometer a geographical tool?'

'No, it refers to a being.'

'Is this being Geometer an evil being?'

'Not at all.'

'Does Geometer sacrifice human beings in Masonic lodges?'

'Not at all.'

'Who then is this Geometer?'

'It is the master designer.'

'I know that freemasons believe in secrecy but tell us who this master designer called Geometer is?'

'The perfect one.'

'Who is the perfect one?'

'The good one.'

'Who is the good one?'

'God.'

'So you agree with me that notwithstanding all the evil that you labeled on the freemasons, they at least have something good in their possession – G?'

'Yes, G is the most important. It refers to the creator of the world. The one who is indivisible ... The one that Muslims call Allah, the one that Christians call God...'

Iscariot was now getting sick with the rambling of this witness. 'Please do not get excited; you have made your point,' Iscariot whispered to himself.

'No further questions,' concluded Magdalene.

'Re-direct?' asked the judge.

What is the use of questions in re-direct, thought Iscariot? This witness had cleared up G but maybe a question could be asked on something else.

Iscariot stood up and asked, 'forget all the questions you were asked on the Geometer. Let me ask you something new.'

'Objection your honor – new evidence-!' slashed in Magdalene.

'Sustained,' agreed the judge.

Iscariot should have expected the objection from Magdalene. Questions on re-direct were restricted to what had been asked in cross-examination. Iscariot looked at Jesus with anger as if he was the cause of the tension he felt.

CHAPTER 83

THE FINAL NAIL

'I call witness number ten your Honor,' said Iscariot.

The witness entered the stadium court and was ready to throw all his frustrations on Jesus.

'What is your name sir?'

'Christian Cox.'

'What do you do for a living?'

'I just lost my job.'

'What happened?'

'I was a preacher but I ceased being a Christian.'

'How did that happen?'

'My whole family was excited about the Da Vinci Code movie and I let them watch it. They came back with strange questions.'

'What did you do?'

'I advised them to read the book.'

'What happened next?'

'Things got worse. Their questions increased and I could not answer any of them. My children simply stopped going to church and accused me of not telling them the truth.'

'What did you do next?'

'I watched the movie again and read the book five times in search of answers. I even tried reading other books like The Shack, Jesus Papers, Jesus the Man but the questions quadrupled. I had enough. I was angry. Very very angry. My mind snapped and I decided to take action and have the man at the centre of the problem arrested. That is how I ended up at Carlifornia police station and demanded that Jesus be arrested.'

'What was your complaint to the police?'

'That Christianity was fake and Jesus was just a fraudster.'

'No further questions.'

CHAPTER 84

I �)(2

Magdalene sympathesised with the witness's complaint. This was an opportunity for her to try and help.

'Are you aware that Jesus was not a Christian?'

'No.'

'Are you aware that Christianity did not exist at all at the time of Jesus?'

'What I know is that Jesus was made God by Christians more than 200 years after his death at Nicaea. I also know that it was the Catholics that were behind all this. Afterall, the first Pope was with Jesus.'

'Who was the first Pope?'

'Peter. That is why I concluded that Jesus created the Roman Catholic Church and Christianity.'

'Would your feelings against Jesus change if you knew that Jesus did not create Christianity and that he was not a Christian at all.'

'Then I would conclude that he is innocent.'

'What is 1+2?'

'Objection your honor, irrelevant,'said Iscariot.

'The relevance will become clear as I proceed your honor.'

'Proceed.'

'What is 1+2?'

'3. That is what the world teaches us from kindergarten.'

'Do you know the mathematics of Jesus?'

'No.'

'Do you know the story in the Bible about the woman who committed adultery?'

'Yes I do. And what I remember most was Jesus writing on the ground.'

'Do you know that what Jesus was writing was 1+2=1?'

'Objection your Honor, opinion evidence. 1+2=1 is opinion evidence.'

'I disagree your Honor. It is not opinion evidence. The author of what was written on the ground is my client present in court with clear instructions on what was written.'

'The prosecutor's objection is overruled,' smashed in the Judge leaving Iscariot frozen.

'1. Do you know that you are good?' Jesus' lawyer proceeded.

'Pardon me?'

'1. Do you know that you are good?'

'Yes I do.'

'2. Do you know that you have the power to be one or not?'

'I know.'

'So if you use 2 to do 1 where do you end up.'

'At 1 of course.'

'No further questions.'

'Re-direct'

'None your Honor,' Iscariot sighed hopelessly kowing that the mathematics of Jesus had finally entered the courtroom.

CHAPTER 85

THE CLOSE OF THE PROSECUTION CASE

'Next witness,' said the Judge as he looked at Iscariot.

'This marks the close of the prosecution case your honor.'

'Any submissions at this stage of the trial?' asked the Judge.

'None,' answered Magdalene.

People were disappointed. This effectively entitles the Judge to put Jesus on his defense. Magdalene could have made an application to have Jesus discharged.

'This is my ruling at the close of the prosecution case,' said the Judge. 'I am satisfied that the prosecution has proved a prima facie case against Jesus. In other words, evidence adduced by the prosecution clearly show that there is cause to put Jesus on his defense and give him an opportunity if he so wishes, to speak for himself.'

The Judge then asked Jesus to stand up.

'You have a right to remain silent. You have a right to call witnesses in your defense. If you choose to say anything you would have to give evidence on oath - yes, Miss Magdalene Royal?' The Judge asked as he saw Magdalene stand up.

'I have instructions from my client that he will give evidence on oath.'

CHAPTER 86

JESUS PUT ON HIS DEFENSE

The crowd in the stadium court clapped and whistled. They shouted, 'Yeshuwa, Yeshuwa, Yeshuwa.' The Umpires had a hard time keeping them quiet. Finally after five minutes of uncontrollable noise, the Umpires cooled the crowd and brought them to a dead silence.

This is what everyone was waiting for; to hear Jesus speak in his defense. The journalists were excited. They would certainly have a lot to report after court hours.

Iscariot too was excited. He saw his dream come true. Finally, he would have a chance to put hard questions to

Jesus, especially the question about Jesus and his secret girlfriend- Magdalene!

Jesus was requested to move from the accused box to the witness box. He stood up, walked slowly to the witness box and waited whilst standing. He was sworn in and everybody waited to hear his defense.

This is what Jesus said.

CHAPTER 87

JESUS SPEAKS

CHAPTER 88

JESUS' DEFENSE

Nothing! Jesus said nothing!

The Judge gave him a minute more hoping Jesus would utter a word.

Nothing.

'This is all in examination in chief,' declared Magdalene.

'Objection your honor, this is a mockery of court process,' puffed Iscariot. 'How can defense counsel claim her client gave evidence on oath when he did not utter a single word?'

'My client did give evidence on oath your honor,' protested Magdalene. 'I do not see any merit in the prosecutor's objection.'

'Your honor,' barked Iscariot, 'I expected my learned colleague to see sense after my objection. This is an abuse of court process. The jurors are being deliberately misled.'

'Your honor, it is the prosecutor who is misleading the jurors-' jumped in Magdalene.

'Approach the bench.' The Judge ordered the two lawyers.

Both Magdalene and Iscariot slowly approached the bench knowing that the Judge was not amused with their fight.

'I do not want this trial to descend into a squabble,' The Judge warned sternly. 'Magdalene, do you have a good explanation why you insist what your client did constitute evidence on oath?'

'I do your honor.'

'Then I will let you explain your reason to the jurors,' said the judge still surprised that Magdalene did not take the scapegoat she was kindly offered.

The Judge then addressed the jurors.

'There is a very important aspect of this trial that has been brought up. You have heard the objection from the prosecution team. The prosecutor rightly wants to know from defense counsel how silence under oath constitutes evidence on oath. Defense counsel will address this court on this subject.'

Magdalene stood up and addressed the stadium court.

'Ladies and gentlemen of the jury, the only person in the stadium court who can give evidence on oath without saying a word is Jesus. The reason is simple. This is a man who died almost two thousand years ago. His presence today constitutes evidence. My client gave me instructions that he would like to give the evidence of his presence on oath as his defense. That is why he was sworn in. All he needed to do was stand in the witness box and be seen. I repeat. His presence in the witness box constitutes evidence on oath.'

Magdalene sat down.

CHAPTER 89

JESUS CROSS-EXAMINED

Iscariot's nightmare was back. This has been the most difficult issue he had to deal with in this whole trial- the presence of Jesus. Who is he to argue against it? He would then be accused of having an innocent man masquerading as Jesus.

'I now understand defense counsel's argument your honor. I withdraw my objection,' conceded Iscariot.

How did he not see that coming? This was certainly very ingenious of Magdalene.

'Cross-examination?' asked the Judge as he looked at Iscariot.

Iscariot stood up still trying to digest what happened.

'Can you explain why you liked kissing Mary Magdalene on her mouth?' asked Iscariot.

'Objection your honor – new evidence,' cried Magdalene.

'Sustained.'

'Did you have sex with Mary Magdalene?' asked Iscariot with hesitation.

'Objection your honor – new evidence,' cut in Magdalene again.

'Sustained.'

'Was Judas influenced by Satan or by you?'

'Objection your honor.' Magdalene was now getting annoyed.

'S-U-S-T-A-I-N-E-D.' stressed the Judge.

'Are you God?'

'Objection your honor, the prosecutor's questions now amount to abuse of court process.'

'Sustained! Learned prosecutor, the only evidence adduced by the accused is his presence. Your questions in cross-examination are restricted to the accused's presence. Any other question would be new evidence and defense counsel would certainly object as you have already seen. Proceed and restrict yourself to the presence of the accused,' lashed out the Judge.

Oh no. Not at all, questioning Jesus' presence was suicide. It was tantamount to succumbing to defeat.

'Your honor, how am I expected to question Jesus when he did not utter a word? Unless I simply tender him in as an exhibit.'

'Do you want to tender him in as an exhibit?'

'Yes… No…No- I mean, yes your honor.' Iscariot answered, clearly confused.'

'Let the record show Jesus as exhibit 2,' ordered the Judge.

'That is the end of my cross examination,' concluded Iscariot.

'Re-direct Miss Royal?'

'No questions in re-direct your honor.'

'Jesus, you are excused from the witness box. You can now return to the accused box. Miss Royal, call your next witness.'

'This marks the close of the defense case your honor,' declared Magdalene.

Both teams then agreed that they would give their closing arguments the next day. Magdalene knew she had ended her case on a very high note. But she also knew that Iscariot fights like a wounded buffalo. He simply never gives up and may make up for what he has lost today in his final address.

CHAPTER 90

Iscariot's Final Address

I scariot knew that what had happened the day before was a serious set back. But he still had confidence that Jesus was going to be found guilty. He put several thousand-page books on his table just to impress the jury. He was prepared for his final address.

'The evidence adduced by the prosecution speaks for itself,' Iscariot started his final address. 'The first witness has shown that a man born just like you and me pretends that he was born of some divine intervention, that some spirit went into Mary and made her pregnant when she was betrothed to Joseph. Is this not adultery? And if it is not adultery, is it not fornication? Does it make sense that God should be accused of adultery or fornication? No, members of the jury, Joseph had sexual intercourse with Mary and that is how this man Jesus was born. His lies about the basic fact of life show a motive to lie.

'The second witness corroborated the first. By corroboration I mean supported. She showed how and why there was a cover up of the truth about Jesus' birth. Now we worship a pagan day, 25th December, and make it into an angelic and heavenly day all because of some conspiracy of Jesus, Judas and others.

'Members of the jury, two witnesses have testified to Jesus' confession of the crimes he is facing. Even if there was no other evidence, the confession itself is an unequivocal admission of guilt. You have heard how Jesus praised Peter for calling him a Son of God. You have heard too how Jesus himself confessed that he was a Son of God. What more do you need? The confession speaks for itself.

'The defense will argue that it is not Jesus but his followers who did all this cover up. My God, that is why this is a conspiracy. Just watching people cover up for you and pretending that you were not physically involved is not a defense.

'You have also heard the facts about Jesus' death-this is the most dramatic. A death like yours and mine is suddenly twisted into resurrection. The facts speak for themselves. Yes, the tomb was empty but empty tomb is not equal to resurrection. The witness who testified to Jesus' death showed how the conspiracy was planned and carried out with Judas Iscariot at the fore front.

'Witness number six, Dr. Nab Nworb, gave evidence on what happened to both Jesus and his secret wife Mary Magdalene after the fake death on the cross. There is no need for me to repeat what he said.

'The seventh witness clearly showed us, not what the Holy Grail is, but who it is. We now know that it is none other than Mary Magdalene's womb carrying Jesus' child.

'The eighth witness testified to how Jesus was elevated from mere man to divinity at the Council of Nicea in 325 AD.

'The nineth witness destroyed G and showed that it was nothing but an evil symbol.

'The tenth witness was the complainant himself who clearly stated how Jesus, the fraudster, as he calls him, destroyed his life.

'Members of the jury, what do we make of all this evidence? Only one conclusion, that Christianity is one gigantic fraud. It is simply a brainwash of the mind and at the center of it is this man Jesus. I believe you will find him guilty on all four counts.'

CHAPTER 91

ⅢAGDALENE'S FINAL ADDRESS

Time had come now for Jesus' lawyer to talk directly to the jurors in her final address. This was what made or broke a case. A lawyer should have the ability to piece together what had happened and convince the jurors that her story should be the basis of their decision and not the opponent's.

'Ladies and gentlemen of the jury, for the first time in the history of the world Jesus has been dissected,' declared Magdalene. 'By dissection I mean thoroughly investigated, tried and tested. We are now in a better position to say with authority whether this man Jesus is the world's biggest fraudster or the world's most innocent man ever tried.

'The prosecution has called a total of ten witnesses. Evidence adduced has proved one thing. That Jesus was fully human. I repeat, not quarter human or half human but fully human, in all things like you and me. 100% human. He too, like you and me, was called to live life according to G. If there is any crime this man committed then it is the crime of living life according to G. Jesus believed in G with all his heart, with all his strength and with all his soul. To him G was everything. G was the key. G was life itself. G was God.

'It is not that only he had G but we have heard from evidence adduced that all human beings, everyone in the world, everyone in this stadium court, have G. What difference is there then between Jesus and all of us? Nothing. We are all the same. We all have G.

'But there is one difference- every one of us has experienced making a decision against G. Everyone of us has done 1+2=3. At that one moment we turned against ourselves and chose that which was not G. That is why Christians say we have all sinned except one. Only one. To Jesus 1+2 was always equal to 1.Only Jesus lived his whole life without abandoning G at any one moment of his life. Jesus always used 2 to chose G. Only Jesus loved G so much that he never ever made any decision that went against G. His mathematics never touched 3.

'Was he not tempted? Did he not feel like giving up G? Did he not feel like G had abandoned him? The Bible speaks for itself. His sticking to G meant insults, mockery, scourging and death but Jesus stuck to it.

'Ladies and gentlemen of the jury, is it a sin to be without sin? Is it a crime to live life without crime? Is it a crime to live like God, to be like God, to be one with God? This man has done what we have failed to do. This man just wanted to be what he was created to be. Like you and me, he was created with the capability not to sin. The fact that he chose to fully use his humanity to live without sin should not make us who have failed to live without sin make him a criminal. If there is anybody who deserves to be in that box, it is you and me, not this innocent man.

'The same we, with our sin, could not believe that a human being, just like us, could live without sin. We went on to create a religion, dogmas and doctrines to justify why this innocent man lived without sin. We added angels, doves and inexplicable miracles to his human story so that we could justify our sin and say he managed to live without sin because he was Son of God. Why not say it the other way round? He was Son of God because he managed to live without sin. I repeat, he was son of God because he managed to live without sin. When called to forgive, he forgave seventy times seven; when called to love, he loved friends and enemies alike.

'We got so amazed that a human being could live like God that we made him God. Yes, WE made him God. Did we have any right to make him God? Yes, we did. We saw in this Jesus a human being who was one and the same with God, a human being who could not be separated from God, a human being who chose not to separate himself from God.

'Jesus did not create Christianity, we did. Jesus did not create the Bible, we did. Jesus did not stand on the hilltops and announce that he was God, we did. All Jesus did is live it. Shame on us for accusing him of claiming to be God. We may have made him God with good reason but leave this innocent man alone. If it ever turned out that our decision that he was Son of God or God was wrong, we should take responsibility of our decision and leave Jesus out of it.

'All he wanted was for us to learn the key to how he successfully lived his life according to G. The hidden key is no one's property. Every human being can find the key. Is this not what we all search for? The key to health, the key to a successful job, the key to a good relationship, the key to life. It is strange that Jesus had the key but Christians lost it. Christianity is supposed to be a religion based on the key and the key is the mathematics of Jesus.

'All he asked was that we follow what he did and the only way to learn the key was to follow him in his commitment to live life according to G. Living according to G is not a message for a particular race, culture or religion. It is a message for every human being. How you express it and what religion you follow matters not, as long as you live your life according to G.

'We even create controversies around Jesus as if controversies are the most important things to him. Do you know how this world would change if we simply do what Jesus wants us to do. No, not create more religions, dogmas and doctrines but just do that which every human being is called to do which is live life according to G.

'I believe, members of the jury, that you will find the accused Jesus innocent of all four counts and acquit him.

'I rest my case.'

CHAPTER 92

JUR⊕RS' DELIBERATI⊕NS

The jurors spent hours deliberating. After intense and highly emotional deliberations the announcement finally came that the jury had reached a verdict. Every one was excited. The time had come to hear how the twelve jurors had decided. It was certainly not a draw; if it were there would be no unanimous decision. What had happened was that six jurors had joined the camp of the other six. The question that remained was whether it was the Christians who capitulated and became atheists or whether it was the atheists who had now become believers.

The foreman was called upon to read the verdict. Ignatius Brown stood up and instead asked for a basin of water. One was quickly brought into the stadium court. Everyone was held in suspense. The foreman looked up to the judge and said something that shocked the whole world.

'We, members of the jury, have decided to wash our hands off the expected verdict,' He declared as the basin was passed from one juror to the other till all the twelve had washed their hands.

'We are only twelve of us,' continued the foreman, 'expected to make a decision that would affect more than half the population of this world. They are over two billion Christians out there to whom the verdict is a matter of life and death. In addition they are over a billion others that believe in Jesus as a prophet. Jesus is therefore a matter of more than three billion human beings as I speak. Who are we, the twelve of us, to decide for the billions? We believe it is prudent that in this information technology age, a better way can be found to pass a verdict on Jesus. Twelve jurors are not enough.

'We the jurors have unanimously agreed that we ask the judge to rule that every human being on this earth be a potential juror. If this court agrees with our request, we ask that the record of this trial be made available to everyone. A web site can be opened to which any person concerned, Christian or non-Christian, can send in their verdict after reading the record of this court. Simple majority rule can be used then to determine if the world considers Jesus guilty or innocent by comparing the number of "guilty" decisions to the number of "innocent" decisions.

'This is our verdict.'

CHAPTER 93

THE JUDGMENT

Strange decision, even the judge was surprised. The judge asked both the prosecution and defense to react to the jurors' verdict.

The prosecution team was excited. They would love to see some web site with millions and millions of people sending in their guilty verdict. After all, their aim was not just to get a guilty verdict in court but get all the over two billion Christians to walk out on Jesus. The best way forward was to give the Christians their chance to walk out on Jesus by sending their guilty verdict to the web site with or without reason. This would certainly destroy Christianity and wipe Jesus out from this earth.

Magdalene too was excited with the verdict. Her thoughts, though, were the exact opposite of Iscariot and his team. To Magdalene, a web site of millions of jurors would show the world how innocent Jesus was. This would clear her client's name.

So both prosecution and defense supported the jurors' motion. What remained was for the judge to give his final ruling that everyone called "The Judgment". A two-hour recess was taken and the court was thereafter reconvened for the final word from the judge. Everyone held their breath as they listened to the judge.

'This is an interesting decision by the jurors,' the Judge said as he started reading his ruling. 'Nothing like this has ever happened in a court of law. Keep in mind though that what the jurors are asking for has a precedent. Jesus himself, the accused in the dock, was tried almost two thousand years ago. Pontius Pilate washed his hands off Jesus' case and it was left to the people to decide. We all know that the shouts of the people that found Jesus guilty and set Barabbas free were not fairly conducted. It was simply mob psychology. There was no scientific way in which one could determine whether the whole multitude considered Jesus guilty. In the end, the Jews were blamed for Jesus' death as if they ALL were given a chance to say whether Jesus was guilty or innocent.

'We are not going to make the same mistake. We live in an age of advanced information technology. With computers and the World Wide Web, we are capable of getting millions of people pass a verdict.

'The world's biggest reality show 'American idol' has effectively used modern technology to get its verdicts. Instead of three judges making the final decision, the people are given the power to decide. 'Big brother', another reality show, has done the same thing. There is nothing to stop this court from doing the same thing.

'I therefore rule in favor of the jurors' motion, supported by both the prosecution and the defense, that all human beings be given the freedom to be jurors in this case and send their verdict to the web site. For information about other ways of sending your verdict like Short Message Settings (sms), log on to the web site. The final decision will therefore be based on simple majority. Write your verdict now and send it.

END OF TRIAL

EPIL⊕GUE

'Arrest Iscariot Jones and release John Puzio,' ordered the police chief.

'Sir, you want to charge Iscariot Jones with a criminal offence?

'No. I want Iscariot Jones to explain, as a witness, his murder of Fr. Perdo and Raymond Brown.'

'You mean as an accused person sir.'

'No, as a witness,' repeated the police chief. 'I want to cut a deal with him to be a witness.'

'I am confused. Who then is the accused if not Jones?'

'The warrant of arrest explains everything. Execute it.'

Officer Saint Christos looked at the arrest warrant with disbelief. He looked at the warrant again and without doubt the order was clear; an arrest warrant for the Devil!

END